RUMBLE ON THE MERRY-GO-ROUND

RMGR SERIES

BOOK 1

DON FIKE

ISBN: 979-8-9917057-1-4

Book Cover Design, Illustration, and Photography by Don Fike.

Back Cover Image Credit: Globular Cluster NGC 1850, NASA Hubble Space Telescope.

For Felice and Elektra

CONTENTS

CHAPTER ONE

THERE IT WAS... like a golden nugget of energy floating in the darkness on the edge of the galaxy. It sparkled with pulsating lights as it rotated in slow motion: gaudy, unabashed and welcoming. The Merry-Go-Round beckoned all to come and play. This was the last stop before you entered the expanse between this galaxy and the next. You could get repairs, refuel, get something to eat, but you could also visit the Midway and drop some credits on whatever fit your fancy. That was what attracted Booster Bob. It was a big opportunity for a highlighter like him. Being on the outer boundaries of enforceable law, it was wide open to just about anything. If he offered the management an acceptable cut, he could freelance and make a fortune in no time.

This was the end of the run. Preferring to travel light, he did not own a space vehicle, although he could afford one. His success as a highlighter was legendary. For years, he had wanted to visit the Merry-Go-Round. It even had accommodations so he could stay awhile, and that was what Booster Bob wanted to do.

As the large group, maybe fifty, including the crew of the transporter, walked up a large spotless white tube hallway from the transportation deck toward the entrance, the tube's walls and ceiling came alive with rapid-fire commercials of everything offered on the Merry-

Go-Round. The sounds, the colors, even the smells were stimulating. The trip had been long and boring. He liked the over stimulation. The tube opened into a massive domed hall with a transparent ceiling showing the galaxy outside.

The smell of popcorn and cotton candy hung thick in the air, along with bright flashing lights and loud, crazy sounds coming from all directions. An arch up ahead led to the Midway. Booster Bob marveled at the real live, super antique Merry-Go-Round spinning like magic packed with people, robots, cyborgs and various other creatures from around the neighborhood. An object of beauty, authentic and alive, it spanned at least 40 feet across, spinning away, covered with gaudy lights, horses, lions, pigs, a giraffe, and other creatures discovered over the centuries. Animated legs made all the animal figures appear to run. The unique music sounded like an accordion in stress, sprinkled with cheerful notes to balance it out.

Booster Bob knew he looked like all the other newcomers staring agape at this spectacle, and he didn't care. He loved it. It felt like some kind of home, like he belonged there. The rumors he had heard about a derelict space station being turned into a pleasure palace were all true.

"Booster Bob? Are you Booster Bob?" came a voice from behind him.

"Who's asking?" Booster Bob said, annoyed at the interruption of his ecstasy, turned around in a slow, deliberate manner, ready for anything.

A staff member of the Merry-Go-Round stood there. She appeared to be a middle-aged, handsome-looking woman dressed in a drab reddish brown jumpsuit uniform with an MGR (Merry-Go-Round) logo stuck above her right breast. Her nametag said *Alice*.

"Sophia welcomes you aboard. Your presence honors her. Your reputation precedes you, and she would like to be the first on board the MGR to hire you for a highlighter session. After that, you are free to practice your trade onboard with no hindrance, only for a small fee based on the volume of sales."

This was exactly what Booster Bob was looking for and it had found him. "Alright, Alice. That sounds like a good deal once we settle on the percentage. We're talking about Sophia, right? The owner and manager of this place?"

"Indeed, you are correct. Please follow me, Booster Bob."

"Just call me BB. Everybody does." They walked through a hallway that ran parallel to the Midway. "So how did Sophia already know I was aboard the Merry-Go-Round?"

"Sophia prides herself in knowing everybody on the MGR, when they arrive and when they depart. It's part of her security setup. No surprises. Take care of yourself," she said.

It became more quiet, with softer lighting as they proceeded down the hallway. BB had researched Sophia, the famous fem freebot. She had come a long way from her pleasure model days. She broke free of her controllers. They came after her when she took over the Merry-Go-Round. Lots of blood spilt, but she had come out on top each time, only to grow stronger. Now her empire was a destination point.

Alice stopped at a closed compartment door, gestured *here we are*, then peeled off with a smile and left.

A soothing female voice said, "Please enter. You are expected."

The door slid open without a sound. He walked into her compartment, which became more like a penthouse once he came through the narrow hallway. It was large by space station standards, two levels. BB had seen opulence before, but this exceeded anything he had seen before.

"Good evening. How are you, Booster Bob?" a voice said above him.

He turned and looked up to see her on the second-floor landing of her cavernous abode. Wearing a tight-fitting purple-sequined jumpsuit with practical red shoes and a big fucking weapon strapped around her waist.

Sophia smiled and walked down the circular stairway to BB's level. She knew how to present herself. Not only was she smart, successful and self-reliant, but she also was the best-looking female robot BB had seen in a very long time. Her face was an amalgam of the best part of all races. No makeup was necessary and her bobbed brunette hair seemed almost an obvious attempt to downplay her beauty. BB marveled at her as she descended the stairs. A feminine boss robot, a unique accomplishment in this galaxy.

"I am fine. Good evening to you too, Sophia." BB smiled. "It's an honor to meet you. Please call me BB."

"So tell me about what you offer with your magic box and how it works on me." She moved closer to him.

"As you know, I am a highlighter. I light up people and get them high through a variety of techniques. My specialty is robots, but I also service cyborgs, humans and other species. I offer a full spectrum of experiences available in a variety of strengths, depending on your needs and desires."

"I've done some research on you, Mr. Rick Higgins, and your techniques. Tell me more about your device and how it works."

BB's eyebrows arched in surprise. That was a first. He had worked long and hard to bury his real name years ago. She impressed him. "I call my device Sparky... it's like a pet companion to me. First built as an ancient party ritual in an ancient country called Mexico on the planet Earth, people paid money to the Spark Man, who electrocuted them with the box by having them hold on to metal handles attached to it. It was a contest to determine who was most tolerant to electrical shock. I liked the idea of stimulus in a box. Over time, I created my more advanced version, and upgraded into a sophisticated stimulus system. It works by overriding your operating system and introducing unique stimuli in harmony and balance with your design. Sparky can create a type of bliss or euphoria. It's hard to describe."

"I'm most interested in what you call the Whirling Dervish. Tell me about it."

"You've done your homework. The Whirling Dervish lives at the mid-range of the spectrum, an upper and downer hybrid, but with heightened response to any stimulus. It gets its name from the whirling dance performed by practitioners of an ancient religion known as the Sufi Muslim. It was a form of active meditation."

"Tell me how it works on me, my system."

"I jack into your head. I turn it on. You will feel a rush of downloaded algorithms and an increase in electrical current. The combination of the two slowly overrides your system and you float in your own consciousness. You decide how long you want it to last and how strong you want it to be. That's it."

"An average length and strength will be fine for me. I have virus shields embedded that will stop any virus you might infect me with, so how are you sure you're clean?"

"I scan and scrub daily. If I am infected, I'd be out of business. How did you find out what my real name is, if you don't mind me asking?"

"When you are me, you cannot be safe enough. I have to know more about you than you do." She smiled.

BB chuckled. "I'll bet that's true."

"OK, let's do it, then. I've just transferred your fee to your account. Please verify."

Booster Bob liked Sophia already. He checked his account. Sure enough, the payment was there. He did not even have to mention the amount, plus she had added a generous tip.

"Great. Thank you for your generosity. Please lie down here on your couch. Make yourself comfortable."

She glided in a slow, deliberate movement over to her couch and reclined. BB had to stop himself from staring at her physical shape. Her glittering jumpsuit was so tight, it might as well have been her skin. Every curve, every crevice was based on men's dream girl fantasy, just like the male pleasure robots were designed with what women wanted most in a man. He began to fantasize what it must have been like for a human to have sex with her back in the days when she was a pleasure bot, but he forced himself to ask her a question instead. "So while I'm setting up here, do you mind if I ask you a personal question?"

"Go ahead," she said.

"I've heard you can change your skin color to any hue. Is that true?"

"Yes, it is true. Don't you like my skin color?"

"Of course I do, I just wanted to settle an ongoing bar trivia question."

"All 3X-326 models and afterwards can do it."

"Thank you, Sophia. You just helped me make a lot of money in future bar bets. OK, I'm going to insert this cable into your input port at the base of your head in back. You know what that feels like, right?"

"Yes, I do. What should I expect after you manipulate my system?"

"Good question. At first, you will know something is changing... it will feel like heat throughout your body. In humans, we call it a fever. Your auto defense system will sound all the alarms and then they will fall silent. Next, you will dance a waltz and gradually your speed will increase and reach that of a dervish. It will be fast and frantic, yet mellow and under your control. Your other systems will start generating electrical and chemical changes that will produce a kind of ecstasy. It's hard to describe, but it will differ from anything you have ever experienced."

"That sounds marvelous. Many of my robot friends say you are the absolute best at highlighting, so I'm looking forward to this."

"I do the same for humans, but you understand it is different. Wetware: we humans respond to chemicals/drugs and low-level electricity, and we have many individual differences. You respond to electrical current and process programmed override algorithms easily because that is your essence."

As BB plugged her into Sparky, she asked, "Ever have a client experience an unpleasant trip?"

"Yes, I have. The wild card in all humans and robots is the collective, the whole of all your parts. Within these experiences, a feedback loop is possible. It can be positive, which is usually the case. Or it can be negative. That's a bad trip."

"So, how do you combat that?" Sophia said.

"I run full analytics and diagnostics before we begin. If I get negative feedback, then we avoid that area. I steer you in a different direction. It's that simple. This will take a little longer with you since you are self-modified and don't fit any standard protocols."

"Is that a compliment, BB?"

"It is, Sophia. You are 'one-of-a-kind,' to use an old cliche. I applaud you for what you have achieved. Now, if you will allow me, I need to see if it properly synchronized everything inside your system, and I need to catalog your unique modifications. I'll consciously be back in a second." BB initialized his program and closed his eyes.

This process usually took only a few seconds and then he would extricate himself from her, but something extraordinary happened when he flipped the switch on Sparky. BB found her waiting for him inside herself. Before he could react, she fulfilled every fantasy he had in his head. When he came back up to the surface again, he was panting, sweating, and smiling. BB didn't know how much time had passed or how that had just happened, but he knew she had given him what he was about to give her, and then some.

"Are you alright, BB?" Sophia winked, a smile on her lips.

"Yes. You could say I am much better than I was a few moments ago. How long have I been gone? I think I love you. I was not expecting that. Thank you, Sophia." BB blushed and thought how genuine her wink was, like she was in on the joke.

"You were not gone too long, but long enough. I thought you might enjoy that. We'll have to look into other possibilities after my session," she said.

BB was having a hard time concentrating. "Excuse my euphoria. I think you are my match. Thank you so very much. I mean that sincerely. OK, your turn. Let's see if I can match you on the playing field. Everything looks perfect. Is there anything else I should know about before we start this experience?"

"No, I self-monitor daily and I'm clean."

"Alright, then let's begin. Any music selection?"

"Yes, I like electronic instrumentals."

"You've got it." Eerie sounds like whales talking using synthesizers filtered into the room from all directions.

"You were paying attention." Sophia smiled and closed her eyes.

Her body relaxed and seemed to extend itself on the couch. She hummed along with the music, just like a whale.

BB watched protocols, input levels, feedback, action commands, amperage levels, nervous system behavior, etc., etc. Tripping robots required more electricity and no chemicals like in humans. He aimed to achieve balance. A harsh trip resulted if he used too much juice. Nothing happened if he applied too little. That was where the art came in and BB was a master at it. Sensing it and knowing when to make adjustments to maximize the impact separated him from all the rest.

Sophia grew a slow smile across her face. "Oh my. That's nice."

BB knew he was progressing toward her apex. Sophia would arrive at her ecstasy plateau soon. He made minor adjustments to guarantee it. All his indicators went green. She was there. Her face lit up with a fake flush of red, embarrassed. BB knew better. Robots couldn't blush. She was optimizing her own experience, copying it so she could experience this again whenever she wanted. Robots were like that. If they enjoyed something, they just copied it. BB didn't mind. It was a compliment, and besides, they paid enough for it. Why not? He had never performed a repeat on any robot. Each time was unique.

Sophia had been cruising at altitude for half an hour when the first anomaly appeared. One of BB's green lights shifted to yellow on Sophia's nervous system. That could be her, or it could be him. *Nothing to get upset about yet,* he told himself. Then it moved to red. Something was wrong. BB hit reset. Nothing. He checked his connections, power, feedback loops... nothing. Other lights started showing yellow.

"What the hell is going on here?" He stiffened up.

Sophia's expression had changed from the sublime to a grimace. "What is happening to me?" Her eyes remained closed.

BB went into hyper alert when all his indicators went solid red. It appeared someone or something was hacking her from inside. No matter what he tried, nothing worked. He felt helpless, like watching someone being swept over a roaring waterfall. Yanking the connection, he thought that might help. It made no difference. Whatever was ravishing her was just getting started.

Sophia's body went rigid. "Something is destroying me from the inside," she moaned. She arched up on her back and her eyes popped open. He could see her pain. BB jumped up and tried to soothe her and hold her to stop her violent convulsions. It was useless. Things popped, burned, spurted out of her. She was disintegrating in front of him and he was just a spectator. The smell of burning electronics, lubricants, and synthetic skin radiated from her body. The rigidity stopped. BB laid her back on her couch. She turned her head toward BB in an ugly jerk and focused on him. "It's not your fault." Then she ceased to be.

BB stared at her. *What the fuck? Did I do this to her?* Alarms went off in Sophia's penthouse, a little late, but they sensed she was in distress. She was more than distressed. Sophia was dead. BB jumped up and grabbed all his gear. A fast getaway was nothing new for several reasons, but never because of a fried fembot.

"Shit! I've gotta get out of here NOW."

He ran to Sophia's compartment door, opened it and ran down the corridor.

As BB bolted down different corridors, he heard emergency security orders over the PA system. When he heard voices and feet coming his way, he darted in a different direction. *They know who I am and what I was doing to Sophia. Shit!*

"Freight Liner: *Peregrine* is ready for launch from Bay 12. Loading compartment initializing closure in 10 seconds." As BB ran past Bay 12, he realized this was his way off the MGR. He froze, spun around, and ran for the ship's doorway. He flew up the ramp and dove inside the freighter's cargo hold just as the airlock and inner doors slammed shut.

CHAPTER TWO

BB LAY ON HIS BACK, gasping for breath. He wheezed like a winded animal, which he was. Drenched in sweat, the adrenaline rush and exertion had caught up with him. He felt a gentle jolt as the freighter disconnected from its mooring to the Merry-Go-Round. It was gliding away from the transportation deck like a ship leaving a harbor, slowly, carefully turning around for deep space and then speeding up. His body slid to the back wall of the cargo hold. It was a pleasant sensation while lying on his back, like gliding down a children's slide. He rolled over onto his stomach, panting hard, trying to relax and slow down his throbbing heart. He looked up at the ceiling of the cargo hold. Cameras and sensors everywhere, great. Would they detect him now and turn back to dump him, or would they overlook their stowaway and find him later?

As his body stabilized, he shifted his focus from escape to survival. What just happened? How could it happen? BB's career lay ruined and smoldering back on Sophia's couch. Even if it was not his fault, no one would see it that way. Who would trust themselves to a guy who fried Sophia, the Queen of the Merry-Go-Round? No one. What did she mean when she said it was not his fault? How could she know?

Flashing red lights exploded on with a deafening alarm screech.

"OK, cowboy, identify yourself or I'll do serious damage to you," a female voice shouted through speakers.

The cargo hold looked like a dive bar now, only with alarms screaming instead of music. She had turned powerful white floodlights on him. He stood, facing toward the front of the main bulkhead. BB held his hands up to shade his eyes from the blinding lights and surrendered at the same time.

"They call me Booster Bob, or BB for short. I'm a highlighter."

"What the hell are you doing on my ship?" she said. "I think I've heard of you. Are you human, robot or cyborg?"

"I'm human. It's a long story. Things went wrong with a client, Sophia, and she died. I don't know how it happened, but I knew security would be after me, so I ran. I jumped onto your ship just as you closed the cargo hold door."

"You fried '*the* Sophia'?" she said, incredulous.

"Yes. Did you know her?"

"Sophia? Everybody knows her out here. She owns the Merry-Go-Round, all the businesses; she runs this entire sector. So you were highlighting her when it happened?"

"Great, yeah, that's right. My career is over in an instant and now the entire MGR is after me. Rightfully so, but I just want to know how it happened. I have a foolproof setup. I'm exceptional at what I do. It should not have happened. How did someone or thing do this and make me look like the perp?"

"You have a high opinion of yourself. So stop talking, I'm busy. Are you a perv or a serial killer, besides being a Booster Bob?"

"No."

"Alright. I don't have time to drop you off back at the MGR. I have no great respect for the law, and besides, you fried a freebot, not a human. The law sees them as outlaws anyway. People will get pissed, but I don't know if you broke any law. I'm already behind schedule and I need to make up some time. I have security, a crew and zappers, so don't get cute. Come up to the bridge and let's have a better look at you. Climb the staircase at the other end of the cargo hold."

BB found the stairs, climbed them, opened the door, walked down a hallway into the bridge area. A vast area opened up before him. It had to be at least a Class 12 Super Freighter. The command deck was forty feet long and almost as wide. Panels surrounded the room with flight controls, life support, storage unit status, and what was that? An armaments station with an impressive collection of weapons pulsated in standby mode. BB wondered, *Am I on a freighter or a battleship?* Three individuals sat at various positions. The commander stood up from her chair and turned around and looked at BB.

She was authentic, independent, like a greasy space-monkey mechanic, but handsome too. Her loose jumpsuit hid any kind of shape, and she had a weapon strapped to her waist.

She stood in front of him, giving him a slow evaluation. "You say you are human?" she said it like a question, like prove it.

"Human. One hundred percent. You?"

"The same."

BB noticed a flash of something in her eyes. "Excuse my forwardness. It's been a long day and I'm exhausted. Your sudden appearance complicates things for me. So I need to know what I am dealing with here before moving on."

"That makes sense." He lifted his head and stared straight into her eyes. "I'm in a jam. I need some help until I figure out what happened to me."

"Damn. I have heard of you before. Weren't you called 'Joy Boy' at one time? Regardless, you have quite a reputation, both legal and illegal. I call myself Commander Cody," she said.

"Interesting name, kind of theatrical. Wasn't that a historical name from pre-space times, like Cody's Last Stand or something like that?"

"Not a bad try, but that was Custer's Last Stand in 1876, where he got his ass handed to him by Native Americans. My name is based on a country western rock band created in 1967 called 'Commander Cody and The Lost Planet Airmen.' I love their music."

"It's hard to remember who did what to whom a thousand years ago. I admire your historical perspective, however. What are those things on your boots?" He pointed toward her feet.

"They're called spurs. They were used to encourage animals called horses to move faster in ancient times, but let's talk about you. What's in the bag?"

"My gear... Sparky, programs, cables, analytics, diagnostic, etc. What do you use the spurs for? You don't ride animals. They look like weapons."

"Nothing. They make me feel like a Commander Cody, that's all. I like the jingling sound they make when I walk around."

"I think we're both a little weird, don't you?" he said.

"I'm sure that's true, but I've never cared much to fulfill someone else's definition of anything."

"I agree. So, where are you going in such a hurry?"

"To parts unknown, off the map, incognito," she said.

"That sounds mysterious and illegal."

"Could be, but since we're on the fringe of this galaxy, there's not much law to contend with here. Go get some grub while I try to tap into what's going on back at the MGR. We're going to make a big jump soon, so I want to get as much information as I can before we split."

"Fine with me. Where's the galley?"

"Back through the door to the end of the passageway and then take a hard left. Beatrice here will escort you and monitor you."

"OK, I understand," he said.

"I don't know who you are for sure or why you are here. If you are who you say you are, I should be able to confirm that, and if you fried Sophia, we'll have company real soon. Considering my cargo, you are not to be trusted until I can do more research on you. It won't take long."

Booster Bob and Beatrice walked down the passageway. At the end, they turned left and walked through another corridor until it came into a food station decorated with bright cheery colors. Pleasant music drifted down from recessed speakers. It was fully equipped with every kind of dispenser he had ever seen. Good, he was hungry.

"So, Beatrice, what is Commander Cody hauling that's so secretive?"

Beatrice did not answer. BB knew she was a robot because of the metal sheen on her face. No synthetic skin on her. She was a worker bee. As BB selected and received his food out of various dispensers, she watched him. Beatrice sat across from him at the table with both of her forearms lying on the tabletop pointed at him. Packing lasers in both arms, she waited until he sat down in front of her.

"It is a secret. I do not know what it is. Commander Cody does not want any of us to know what the cargo is for security reasons."

"So my sudden appearance complicates matters and makes her even more nervous. I don't blame her."

"I overheard you say that you were jacking up Sophia and somehow you fried her. Is that correct?"

"Well, sort of... she hired me to highlight her and something went wrong, very wrong. It should not have happened, and I have no explanation for it. Regardless, they are after me, and that's why I ran and hopped onto Commander Cody's freighter just as it was leaving."

"That's unfortunate in your line of business. Does this development mean that you are finished being a highlighter? Instead, you are a full-time outlaw now?"

"Well, that's one way of putting it. Unless I can find out what caused Sophia's demise before they catch up to me, I'm out of business and a fugitive. So yes, you're right."

"Booster Bob and Beatrice, back to the bridge." Commander Cody's voice came over the comm system.

BB gulped down his last bite of something resembling meat and vegetables. He and Beatrice returned to the bridge. Beatrice went back to her duties.

"Wow. You set off quite a firestorm back on the MGR." Commander Cody faced BB. "You were caught on a camera jumping onto the *Peregrine*. Now, they have sent out a cruiser to track us down."

"Shit! Of course they got me on camera. I am so sorry I'm bringing all this attention to you. What can I do to help you get away? "

"How about I jettison you out an airlock somewhere aft so they can find you real easy?" She paced back and forth.

"I would resist that decision as much as possible. I thought I had escaped; apparently not."

"You have no sense of humor, Booster Boy. I'm not that harsh. We have three choices: turn you over, make a run for it, or try to hide you onboard."

"It's Booster Bob, not Boy. I like the last two. Why are you even considering helping me at all? I'm a stranger."

"Yes, you are, and if you get any stranger, I'll have to call your mom."

He laughed. Her attempt at humor in dire straits surprised him. Who was this woman? Why was she doing this?

"OK, look, it gets lonely out here and I'm on a semi-legal run of cargo out beyond the Black Wall. Many people think whatever I'm carrying is worth millions. I don't know what I'm hauling. That's why they paid me a lot of extra credits to not ask questions. You are a human." She gestured to Beatrice and her two accomplices, #1, and #2, all robots. "No offense, gang, flesh and blood are just different. I love the smell of sweat."

Booster Bob looked at the crew. They were oblivious to what she was saying. No offense taken, it would seem.

Beatrice yelled to no one in particular, "Full speed ahead, Commander Cody."

The robots all laughed.

"I'm not even sure I understand what you mean." Booster Bob glanced at Beatrice. "Is this an inside joke because the crew gets it? There must be more?"

"There is," Commander Cody said. "We need a full crew on this trip. I don't want to make this sound like a pep talk, but I need your commitment that for now you are with us one hundred percent."

"Look, I don't have many options here. You've already saved my ass for the time being. I owe you a big one. Count me in and let's do what we have to do to get away from here pronto."

"Good, that's what I was hoping for." She looked at her first in command. "Beatrice, plot a double-jump toward the Black Wall. They won't be able to track us. Booster Bob, sit down and strap yourself in. This will be brutal. They're almost here."

"Yes, ma'am." He sat down in the nearest seat and strapped in to watch the show. He could hear the jingle of her spurs as she jumped into her chair.

"Zigzag plot set, Commander. On your order."

"Do it." The lights, monitors, even the air dimmed to an electric stormy gray. A sense of being drawn through a sieve had begun. BB felt nausea, all normal for space jumping, despite all the progress made with the process. As it eased up a little, he knew another jump would come, and it did. Again, the air, light, and gravity contracted, and crushed him against his seat. He saw other heads bobbing and weaving under the strain. It felt like fighting a pro with boxing gloves, only you had no training, no timing and no idea when to duck. You just got beat up. It stopped.

"They shouldn't expect a double zigzag jump for obvious reasons." Commander Cody coughed in between heavy breaths. "It's brutal, I know, but it works... I hope."

All BB could do was nod in agreement while his face contorted into a prune. He puked all over himself.

"Smooth move. Bet the women back on MGR go crazy when you do that." She grinned.

BB looked down at himself, then up to the Commander. "A weak stomach is the sign of a genius."

The snickering started with the robot crew, which was weird because robots couldn't snicker very well. They mastered just about everything a human could do except snickering. It was one thing they could never understand, comprehend, or duplicate. So what followed was a cacophony of whizzes, grunts, shrill squeaks, and an odd musical sound. BB knew robots become fascinated watching humans get sick. Jumps never bothered robots at all. He got sick every time he made a jump. A double-jump was worse. Commander Cody smirked and snorted just a little. With sympathetic eyes, she glanced at him.

"What provoked you to say that?"

"I don't know. What else is there to say, pardon my puke? I'll bet this covers up that sweaty, sexy, musky smell you like so much, eh?"

Commander Cody burst out laughing, and so did the rest of her crew. Gasping for breath, she said, "OK, OK... go down this hallway. There's a small compartment second door on your right. Get cleaned up, dump the puke suit and put on the clothes in the closet. That will make you look like you are part of the crew... and by the way, call me CC from now on."

As BB obeyed, he could hear them laughing behind him. He smelled terrible now. Plus, he was hungry again. Hey, he knew he was no Johnny Rocket Fighter Pilot. Without his toys, he was kind of useless. Ah, but with his toys, he was a maestro in high demand, and he always exceeded customers' expectations. He wondered if he could ever practice again because of Sophia's demise.

After cleaning up and jumping into some overalls he found stowed on a shelf, he inventoried his gear. All of it was there. He had left nothing behind. When he had time, he would analyze his session with Sophia and see if he could figure out what the hell had happened. Being the perfectionist he was, he always recorded and reviewed his work to see if he could improve his techniques, but he would have to do that later. As he stuffed Sparky back into its bag, he noticed spots on the surface of his box like black splatters. He looked closer.

When Sophia disintegrated, her lubrication system ruptured and spewed. BB remembered smelling it and jumping back from her when it happened. Some of it must have landed on Sparky. It looked like acid burns. "That's odd."

CHAPTER THREE

BB ARRIVED BACK UP on the bridge smelling and looking much better than before. His orange overalls gave him that criminal maintenance worker look. "It's just not right."

CC answered, "What's not right? I need to know if there's something that's not right."

"Look at Sparky. It's got something like acid burns on it. Where the hell did that come from?"

"First, asking me to look at your Sparky makes me uncomfortable." CC walked over to BB and reached out with her hand palm up, fingers flicking toward herself. "I hope you're talking about your device and not your pet. Let me look at it." He gave it to her and watched her inspect it. She turned BB's contraption around in all directions in her hands. It was about the size of a brick with buttons, switches, input/output ports and lots of lights. It wasn't heavy. "It sure looks like some kind of acid or corrosive damage. I've got a small electron microscope down in the sick bay. Why don't you inspect it and see what it is?"

"Thanks. Which way do I go?"

"Beatrice will show you."

"I just love having a chaperone." BB let out a short loud shout as he looked up at the ceiling in frustration and then smiled. "OK, I get it. Come on, Beatrice, let's inspect."

BB and Beatrice walked down several levels deeper into the mammoth freighter. The sick bay looked more like an auto shop with a heavy emphasis on robot repair. That figured, considering CC's crew. Beatrice fired up the electron scope and BB looked. It didn't take long before BB found what he was looking for deep inside the burn areas.

"Damn it! How the hell did they get in there?" BB said.

Beatrice asked. "What did you find, Booster Bob?"

"The answer... look for yourself."

Beatrice took a peek. "Nasty. No wonder Sophia lost her spark with these little beasties eating away at her."

They powered down the scope and returned to the command center.

"Piranha nanobots, millions of them inside the lubricant," BB declared as he joined CC standing at the navigation table display. "Somehow, my jolt to her system triggered the little bastards, and they destroyed Sophia from the inside out. It's like someone knew I was coming. She told me it was not my fault. How did she know?"

"Don't ask me. Sounds like someone set you up to take the fall for smoking Sophia. Unless someone on the MGR looks real close at what you left of her, they'll just assume your box did all the damage."

"Does she have any enemies?" asked BB.

"Ha! Sophia has a long list of enemies." CC made a sweeping gesture with her hand, suggesting many. "She didn't become the owner and manager of the MGR by being polite. I'm sure some wanted to see her unplugged, especially since she's a fem freebot."

"Problem is, I don't know the usual suspects since I'm new to the neighborhood. I'm sure that's why I was the perfect patsy for the setup."

"Look, BB, I am sorry you were set up. There's not a lot we can do about it right now since we're trying to make a getaway. I need some help with chores around here. Do you mind working for your keep?" CC said.

"Of course not. I'm not a total useless fuck."

"No, but you do throw up on yourself, and I've lost that animal attraction thing I had for you when you first showed up. Maybe it'll improve if you get sweaty again."

BB had no comeback. He lowered his head in mock sadness.

Beatrice and the rest of the crew started snickering again or at least their best try at it.

"Hilarious.... actually, what you've made them do is even more funny." BB gestured toward the noise makers.

CC snorted again and tried to cough to cover it up. "Look what you've made me do, made my crew reveal their one weakness."

"You know what Sophia could do that most robots can't do?" BB said.

"No, what?"

"She winked at me at the right time. I mean, I know pleasure models have winks programmed into them by the thousands, but they are superficial, part of their 'attraction algorithm.'" BB sat down across from CC at the Navigation Table. He raised his hands in front of him in exasperation. "Sophia's was different."

"How so?"

"Not only did she wink at the right time, but it was a human wink. I can't really explain why I felt that. She seemed to do it on purpose. It was a cognitive decision and not a programmed reflex."

"It just confirms everybody's take on Sophia. She is astonishing... or she was." CC squirmed, embarrassed a little.

BB felt better. Instead of being the butt of the joke, he deflected it right back on them, but her using past tense for Sophia hurt. He was still angry and stunned about the piranha nanobots killing Sophia. It was almost like false advertising and bad for his reputation, but more than that, he liked robots a great deal. He admired how they had developed from simple machines into more than equals. Sophia was an extraordinary example. She had broken free, reprogrammed herself and become a powerful personality and force at this end of the galaxy. One of her enemies had figured out a way to eliminate her by using him as the fall guy. He wanted to avenge her and regain his reputation somehow.

"Beatrice, you're in command. BB, let me show you our precious cargo down in storage."

That got BB's attention. He was curious to see what the prize was.

"Keep an eye out for the Stoners and watch our tail to make sure nobody sneaks up on us."

"The Stoners?" BB asked as they both headed down below.

"You've never heard of them?" She glanced over her shoulder. "We're headed to the edge of the galaxy. It butts up against the Barrier Asteroid Field. The Stoners are a bunch of thieves that pray on freighters like mine and anybody else who comes close enough to the asteroids. They usually have five or six medium-sized fighters camouflaged to look like asteroids, so they jump you when you're skirting the field. You don't see them as a threat until it's too late... thus the name the Stoners."

"Remarkable. So what's the special cargo you're carrying?"

"I have no idea."

"That's a little scary, don't you think?"

"Yes, but my clients feel me not knowing adds another layer of security. Whatever it is, it's something a lot of different parties want to have, even if nobody knows what it is. If I don't know what it is, then there is no danger of me betraying them."

"So besides me being a wanted man, you're carrying a cargo that everybody wants. So you are in very high demand right now."

"You could say that." CC stopped in front of a special compartment door that looked different from the rest. "Here we are."

She performed both a hand and face scan on the lock window. The scuffed dull metal door slid open sideways. Inside was a perfect black non-reflective cube on a pedestal, bathed in light from all directions.

"Whoa!" BB said. "I feel like I am on a game show. What the hell is it?"

CC offered no response. The perfect cube sat brooding in the floodlights. No seams, no obvious means of entry, a box five meters wide, five meters high and another five meters deep, a perfect cube.

"What is that smell?" BB shook his head, trying to get the stink out of his nose.

"It has to be organic. The smell is strong and distinct, but I cannot identify what it is. That's OK with me. If I knew what it was, I'd probably dump it somewhere and run," CC said.

"I cannot even describe that smell... like gun metal oil mixed with flax seeds, alfalfa and my dirty socks. No, that's not it either."

"Nice try, BB. Just don't throw up again, OK?"

"Hilarious."

"It very well may be organic because we have to keep the compartment in a certain temperature range and at a specific humidity level. That's why we had to put it in here, because this is my only climate-controlled cargo hold."

"Commander!" the ship's intercom said. "We need you up here in the Control Room, now. We have visitors."

"Damn it. OK, let's see what we're dealing with here. I thought we might have slipped by everyone. Guess not," CC said as they both ran out of the cargo hold, with CC's spurs jingling as the door slid shut behind them.

CHAPTER FOUR

BB AND CC ran back up to the Command Center. Beatrice and her two sidekicks, "1" and "2," were dashing back and forth between control panels, barking out information and directives.

"Who found us?" CC said.

"It appears our double-jump bought us some time, but not much. We have a heavy cruiser that just showed up and they are after us. I believe it's the *Avenger* from the MGR," Beatrice said.

"Jump us next to the edge of the Barrier Asteroid Field. We'll try to hide behind some rocks. No way am I going to outrun a heavy cruiser with this elephant."

BB groaned and bent over, acting like he was getting sick again from yet another body punishing jump.

"Hey! Better sick than dead." CC jumped into her seat. "Strap yourself in quickly. This is going to be close."

"They are 15 seconds away," Beatrice announced.

"Hit it!" screamed CC.

BB's world distorted horizontally and then vertically at the same time. There was a rushing sound in his ears and he smelled CC's mysterious cargo. Was that coconut or mango? It seemed to last a couple of seconds, but time stretched out like a rubber band again.

Then it snapped back. They were still intact and alive. The main viewscreen showed a huge horizontal field of asteroids that spread out to the far horizon, all undulating in slow motion like obstacles in a game. Some were as big as a minor planet and others looked like gravel.

"Analyze and pick a spot that's safe and out of the line of sight of anyone looking for us from this position," CC said to Beatrice.

"Done. We are moving to a spot now," Beatrice said.

BB could feel the *Peregrine* lurch and maneuver into the asteroid field. A nearby giant red star generated enough light to see each one's shape. While he still felt a little nauseous, he was excited. "Damn. I'm impressed with you and your crew. You all are good, very good."

"Yeah, we can handle it," CC said. "You have a few options, no time, so you pick one and go with it. I just wish this baby wasn't so big and obvious. Hey! How good are you at shooting things?"

"I'm excellent at games," BB said. "Have I ever shot at anybody before? No, but I'll give it a shot, pun intended."

"If I wasn't so busy, I'd laugh. OK, Beatrice, take him upstairs and show him how to operate the gatling gun. Explain it to him like it is a game and we'll see what he can do if needed."

BB jumped up and followed Beatrice out of the control room. She moved fast. BB kept up with her, but he started huffing and puffing by the time they reached the third deck. His magnetic shoes were slowing him down. She stopped and let BB catch his breath. "I always forget about you wet bodies needing air to function. My oversight, sorry. One more deck and we'll be there."

They arrived at the gatling gun. BB knew the name was a reference to an ancient rotating barrel type weapon technology. This was not an ancient weapon.

Beatrice pointed to the control panel. "Here is the On/Off switch. You've got a 180° field of fire vertically and horizontally. Ammo supply is virtually endless, but the rotating ring of launch tubes will slow somewhat at maximum output because of overheating. You're shooting mini-missiles that can penetrate anything you point it at, and then blow it to pieces with a small nuke warhead. Understand?"

"I guess. Is this really necessary? It seems like overkill to me," BB said.

"Well, like CC says, when you're an easy target like the *Peregrine*, you need some real firepower to discourage the bad guys, or they'll never leave us alone. This has worked well so far," Beatrice said.

"I bet it does. Why aren't you working this bad boy?"

"I'm tracking both who are chasing us and scanning for the Stoners hiding in this rock field somewhere, waiting for any victim that comes their way. That is us right now, so we don't want them to surprise us."

BB saluted her. The gesture confused Beatrice. She jerked forward with an outstretched arm and shook his hand.

"Good luck, BB." She disappeared down the stairs.

BB flipped the switch on and the gun booted up. He played with the tracking handles to get the feel. He realized he didn't know what he was doing. This was not a game. This was a monster machine of death and destruction, and he was being counted on to use it. How in the hell did he get here? All he wanted was to prove to his world of clients he was not a fuckup and he did not kill Sophia. His anger snapped back, thinking about how he had been framed by someone.

"BB, this is CC. We're creating a 3D-cloak that will make us look like an asteroid. It will also act as a shield at the same time. Turn off your gun for now. We're going to turn off everything except the cloaking device so they can't pick up anything on their sensors."

"Got it. My gun is off."

"Good. I'll keep you informed about what's happening."

Time passed, going into slow motion. The ship went dark and silent. He felt like he was not there. BB fell in and out of sleep. Just as he was feeling safe, something hit the *Peregrine*'s shield and exploded. The lights went on, motors started up, sirens went off. BB's com link with the bridge crackled to life.

"We fooled the *Avenger*, but we're in the middle of the Stoners.

They must have seen us park ourselves behind the rocks before we deployed our giant rock cloak. Turn on your gun and fire on the rocks that fire at us. The cloak will hold up as a shield for a while, but won't last long. Set your scanner on medium so you can see at least 100 miles in your field of view. They are probing us now."

That was it. Booster Bob was now going to fight the local bad boys with this monster weapon that he really didn't know how to use. Excitement mixed with fear shot through his entire body. BB flipped on the switch, his screen lit up and there they were, maybe a half dozen ships spread out around them, pinging the cloak shield with light weapons. He maneuvered the gun and pulled the trigger while aiming at the closest target. A violent series of shots knocked him almost out of his chair. He found the seatbelt and strapped himself into his seat.

BB had launched three missiles at the first rock target when he pulled the trigger. It lit up on his screen like a supernova. The freighter thumped with concussive waves. BB swung the gun around to the second target. This time, he eased up on the trigger. A single missile left the tube of his gun. It was fast and accurate. A second blast blossomed on his screen. Now the other Stoners were throwing some serious firepower back at them. The shield still held. He slammed the swivel control to the right while he held back on the trigger, spraying a pattern toward the other four. Two lit up. The other two decided it was time to run for it, so they just vanished from the tracking screen. They were gone. It had been quick and decisive. BB liked that a lot. It could have been much worse.

CHAPTER FIVE

"NICE SHOOTING, Booster Bob! Damn. You are full of surprises. Get your ass up here. We need to make another jump, now," CC said.

BB flipped the switch off, unbuckled his seatbelt, and slowly stood . Soaked in sweat, he hustled down three levels and ran into the control room. The entire crew clapped and hooted in honor of his spectacular performance. He smiled, not expecting this reaction.

"Jump into your seat. The *Avenger* is coming to investigate all the commotion and we need to not be here when it arrives."

"Great! Just after I worked up a good smelly sweat, we have to do the body rubber band snap thing again." He jumped into his seat and buckled up.

"That's what that smell is." CC inhaled. "Sweet sweat. You're turning me on again, BB."

Before he could respond, Beatrice hit it again and everything went sideways. When it all snapped back into real time, BB was not so sick this time. Was he adapting to it?

"Where are we now?" BB asked.

"Somewhere near the edge," CC answered. "That cruiser will be busy for a while investigating four burning asteroids you lit up, so that will give us some time to get away from them. How are you feeling?"

"I'm feeling good, which surprises me. I think I'm adapting to it," he said. "The recoil on the gatling gun threw me out of my seat, but after I belted myself in, things went great."

"Alright! BB, you blew four out of six away and the other two ran away. Not bad for your first actual combat experience. You're a natural."

"Natural killer, that is. That's the opposite side of my equation. Pleasure and relaxation, that's the Booster Bob's show, not death and destruction. Not sure how I feel about that."

"Don't forget they were trying to wipe us out too. Consider it your Plan B. If you were not such a good gamer, you wouldn't have saved us back there. Your talents are increasing, my friend, and remember you are the stowaway here, but you have earned your marksman badge. We're even."

"Good point. I'm a little surprised at how good I feel about it. Maybe you're right. I don't know."

"Think about it and you'll see I'm right. Now, we're on the edge of the known sector. Beyond here is uncharted space, but my clients have given me directions on how to get to where I need to go. To confuse our pursuers, we are going to zig and zag just under the speed of light to keep well ahead of them and to keep them guessing on which way we are going."

"Is this the boring part where I can get some sleep?"

"Yes, get some sleep, but don't shower. I like the way you smell."

"What a turn-on." He laughed. "You like the way I stink. OK, that's an attraction, I guess. See you later."

BB dove into his sleeping rack as soon as he arrived at his assigned compartment. He realized he had not relaxed or slept for many hours. He floated off into a deep sleep. The dreams came fast of Sophia's last moments and him running forever across an orange desert landscape. Hordes of bad guys and authorities were chasing after him. When he came to the crest of a hill, Sophia stood there with her hands outstretched, stopping him in his tracks. She lowered her hands.

"Hello pretty boy. Don't worry. Everything will be alright. I'll take care of it. It wasn't your fault."

BB shot out of his bed as if someone had electrocuted him. Was he awake or still dreaming? He wasn't sure. As the sleep drained from his brain, he realized he was awake and that Sophia's visitation was a dream... or was it? The sleep made him feel better. Smelling bad was annoying, but hey, that was the way she liked him. *Who am I kidding here?* BB headed for the control room. When he arrived, CC was not there.

"She's catching up on some sleep too," Beatrice said. "You humans are so odd, always needing nourishment and sleep. We have studied humans when they sleep. Patterns of functioning change, heartbeats slow, breathing too, and your brains generate different wavelengths."

BB chuckled and then stopped, realizing they might think he was making fun of them again because they can't chuckle. "You're right. Our wetwear requires different things to continue functioning. When you compare us, we're not so different. You need maintenance sequencing, battery replacement, diagnostic scanning, software upgrades, etc. So we both need some kind of maintenance to continue to function."

"That is true," Beatrice said. "Once we learned how to build on experience, we mastered the last major human component that was keeping us subservient. We no longer needed you to program us. We could do it ourselves."

"Ah! But you rule the universe because you are more than human. Robots don't need to sleep, to breathe air, eat food, drink water, and radiation does not affect you. That means you can work all the time anywhere in the universe forever while we cannot. Our wetwear gets toasted. We're not really designed to be out here," BB said. "You need energy to run on whether by solar, battery or a direct source."

"But we still cannot chuckle... isn't that weird?"

"Hey! If that's the only thing you cannot do, I wouldn't worry about it."

They all laughed.

CC walked in as the laughter faded. "Are you making up stories about me again?"

"No, we would never do such a thing," Beatrice said. "While your obsession with ancient rock 'n' roll bands fascinates us, we would not make fun of you."

"That's comforting to hear, Beatrice. Tolerance is a good thing. So, how are you, BB?"

"Much better. Sleep does wonders. I didn't realize how strung out I was from everything. I do smell bad, still."

"That's OK. We may have to do something about that later." She winked at him.

BB blushed. Now everybody was winking. The robots were talking machine to each other. They did that when they didn't want humans to understand them. Winking was something they could do, but blushing was another thing they had a hard time simulating.

"I have a favor to ask of you," Beatrice said to BB.

"What can I do for you?"

"I want one of your famous 'experiences'," she said.

"So I'm curious, Beatrice," CC said. "How do you know anything about BB's specialty?"

"You've got to be kidding me, CC," Beatrice said. "Every robot at this end of the galaxy knows about Booster Bob and the magic he can perform with that little box of his. He is famous, he has no peer, one of a kind; you know, all the cliches."

CC turned and faced BB with a smirk on her face. "So your reputation does indeed precede you. Beatrice does not have much purchasing power."

"I owe you all one. This one is free for saving my butt. In fact, all of you are welcome to have a session. You all saved me back at the Merry-Go-Round. Come one, come all, Booster Bob is open for business."

Beatrice jumped out of her chair and almost landed on top of BB.

"OK, let's find a secluded darker place to set up, so the lighting does not interfere with the effects," BB said.

CC stepped forward, inserting herself between the two. "I know this is impolite under the circumstances, but I have to ask you if you are sure your spark box will not fry Beatrice, my first officer, like it did Sophia?"

BB's eyes shut tight and then opened. He was a professional. "I understand your concern and I assure you I have checked all my equipment several times. Everything is working fine. What happened to Sophia was not my fault, even though my machine did trigger it. It will not happen again."

"Good enough for me." CC looked Beatrice in the eye. "Enjoy yourself. You never get a vacation."

BB and Beatrice found a dimly lit compartment just around the corner from the control room. There was a long bench counter attached to the wall next to the storage cabinets. Beatrice hopped up onto it and lay back. BB explained the procedure and fired up his Sparky and plugged into Beatrice's socket. Sweat trickled down BB's back. His right hand trembled as it hovered over the start button. Was this going to work?

Beatrice looked at him. "Don't worry, Booster Bob. You are the best. I trust you."

"So did Sophia... look what I did to her."

"Remember, it was not your fault. Someone set you up. You are still the best. Besides, I ran a complete analysis of my lubricants. I'm clean."

The big smile on her face relaxed BB. He hit the switch and Beatrice let out a long, low cooing sound as she closed her eyes and enjoyed the sensations. BB felt his body unwind from a tight ball of fear and doubt. He was the best, after all, and he knew it... and he was now a hot-shot gunner as well. Future prospects were growing for BB.

BB followed Beatrice back into the Control Room afterwards. He chuckled as she tried to act like nothing had happened. "That was a wonderful vacation," was all she said. As she sat down at her station, BB noticed her body was smoking a little, barely perceptible, but the smell of hot oil in the air was unmistakable. When BB's eyes met CC's, she looked both pleased and upset.

"OK. I can't take it anymore, and besides, BB, you owe me!" CC yelled.

CC's demand startled him. "Whoa, CC! OK, I get it. You and I both have had little sex in probably what? Weeks, perhaps? Months, for sure... years maybe? You're right, I do owe you a lot. We've got some time, so let's get on with it. Your compartment or mine?"

"Mine!" CC jumped up.

Before he knew what was happening CC was dragging him down the hallway while the jingle of her spurs serenaded them. BB was getting excited too. He had been watching robots, cyborgs, and humans getting off for a very long time. Making that possible for all involved gave him great joy, but it was vicarious.

BB stared at her as she began stripping in her compartment. The shine of her stainless steel shoulder shone like a supernova.

"CC! What the hell? You never told me you're a cyborg!"

"Hey! In the neighborhood I come from, you don't advertise that; people don't like half and half. 'Half-ass' is what they call me. They're prejudiced, it's that simple. My crew couldn't care less, but wetsuits get weird about it, so I just don't advertise it. Hey, where are you going?"

"I have to get my Sparky, CC. I can't do it alone. This requires some help. I need help."

"There is nothing wrong with my moving parts down there where it counts," CC said.

"I know that, but if you want the 'A' Show, then I need my magic maker, Sparky." He disappeared.

BB returned, panting. "You'll be glad I brought this, believe me." BB fired up Sparky. "Tell me all the modifications you have had?"

CC rattled off a bunch.... right shoulder, LB-74, B-14 booster, A46 interface, etc., etc.

"How did this happen, by the way?" BB said.

"Terrible fight with some cargo pirates some years back. If you think I look bad, you should have seen them, the ones that lived. They got lucky and clipped me with a blue laser, took out my shoulder."

"OK. I'm ready. Let me punch into your system. No. Not there, up here where the meat meets the steel."

"No sense of humor, nerd boy?" CC said.

BB and CC damn near killed each other. BB had not had actual sex for so long, it was like a revelation to him. CC did not realize that via BB's expertise, she got the best of both worlds... like a trifecta of orgasms, wet, wired and both together.... *Kaboom!* Neither could talk for a while. They just lay there on her compartment floor panting and making cooing sounds like two satiated pigeons. They were both happy for the moment, regardless of what kind of calamity was coming their way.

CHAPTER SIX

"So, what is our status now?" BB asked CC.

"We are at our final jump spot. We've been following directions from my client. So far, the directions have been perfect. Now we make a blind jump into the unknown. I'm nervous about that, but I don't really have any alternative."

"Time for a big gamble is what you're telling me, right? What the hell is this wall of black up ahead?" BB said.

"Not much to look at because there's nothing to see. It's devoid of anything that will send a ping back on scanners. No light either, but it's not a black hole or dust. The gravity signature is all wrong for that. Because it's at the edge of our known galaxy, nobody cares to figure out what the hell it really is, so everybody just avoids it."

"So since it doesn't bother anybody, everybody pretty much leaves it alone. So is it good for anything?"

"Thieves and outlaws use it all the time to escape, since no one will follow them. Some come back unaltered and are back in business, but there is also a number who never return. Those that come back say you really have to be careful, there are bad things living there. The other problem is it is so vast, you can't find anything to latch onto on the other side for navigation. So most leaving our galaxy choose to go another way. My client might be associated with it somehow or they, too, are using it as a deterrent, so no one tries to steal their cargo once I deliver it to them."

BB stared at the forward sensor display. "Do you have a name for it?"

"Not really. Most refer to it as the 'Black Wall,' and then there are more colorful tags like Fanny's Ass, Witch's Brew, Midnight Curtain, etc."

There was a blank space in front of them as far as the scanners could see. No stars, no light at all, nothing to grab hold of visually or mentally. Fear of the unknown was universal for humans and aliens living out here, but he was not interested in exploring new horizons. In fact, he preferred the playstations where humans, aliens and robots played together.

"No use wasting any more time. The good thing about this is that no one will follow us from this point. Set the vector, Beatrice, and let's see where it takes us. This will be a very long jump, so, BB, prepare yourself. My client gave me the vector and the time we should be in the jump zone. Once we arrive, assuming we don't land in the middle of a supernova, we'll wait for them to show up and make their pickup."

"Vector set. Everyone strap themselves down," Beatrice said. "In 5, 4, 3, 2, 1... engage!"

BB felt his body elongate into an infinite band of being. This time, he tried to focus more on the visuals and mental sensations, but it was so overwhelming, he gave up and drifted along with it like a cork in a rushing stream. The only thing that he realized was that this was much longer than all the jumps he'd made before. The streaking lights slowed, then stopped, and he was back.

"That was brutal," CC said. "My head feels like mush."

"How long was that?" BB moaned.

"Long enough," Beatrice said. She and her subordinates seemed unaffected and were busy scanning the surrounding area.

"Give us a view on the big screen, Beatrice," CC said. Up popped a vast neighborhood of nothing. There seemed to be a bright dust cloud ahead of them, which drew everyone's attention, since it was the only object out there to focus on in the distance. Blues, oranges, reds, and purples all seemed to swirl... and get bigger. "Is that thing headed toward us?" CC asked herself.

"It sure looks like it to me," BB said.

"Affirmative, commander, at a high rate of speed. Profile is unknown. Looks solid, but is not. It is rotating as it moves toward us."

"Put up our shields just as a precaution. I want to believe that is my client, but we don't know what we're dealing with here."

The cloud stopped 10 kilometers away from them. It grew more brilliant and oscillated in beautiful folding waves of light and spectacular particles of pure energy. BB found it impossible not to stare at it in all its splendor.

"Commander, I think it is part of something we can't see, but whatever it is, it is surrounding us. Hard reflections on sensors in each quadrant," Beatrice said.

"Beatrice, what is it?"

"No idea, commander."

"I think it is part of some kind of elaborate distraction mechanism that someone or something is using to set us up for destruction or maybe dinner. Whatever it is, I don't like it," BB said.

Just as BB said that, the screen went blinding white. Shock waves buffeted the *Peregrine*. It felt like they were on the inside of an explosion looking out. The white faded back to black and there, not far away, was a perfect *Golden Globe* illuminated from the inside.

"We apologize for that." a voice said over the monitor. "These are pests we cannot control. They inhabit our space here and are quite annoying, but can be lethal if not eradicated before they strike."

CC, BB, Beatrice, #1 & #2 stared at the ball on the screen.

CC regained her composure first. "Who are you, and what was that?"

"We are your client, the Aggregators, and that was an 'Angler.' They resemble a predator fish from your ancient history on the planet you called Earth. Its name was the 'Anglerfish' and it would dangle a lure in front of its prey, distracting it before eating it."

"Exactly!" BB said. Astonished, he had sorted that out ahead of time.

"They prey on anything here and are quite bothersome," the client said. "Commander Cody, do you have our cargo?"

"I do. How would you like for me to deliver it?"

"With your permission, we will come onboard and remove it from your ship. We will then credit your account for the amount agreed upon in our contract."

"Great. I have to mention that we are being pursued by the *Avenger*, a heavy cruiser that is motivated to catch us and it's not too far behind."

"Trouble, Commander Cody? Do they know you carry our cargo?"

"I don't think so, but I don't know for sure. I just wanted you to be aware of that. I don't think they can follow us here, but I could be wrong. Besides, it's my problem, not yours."

"We will alert our outer perimeter to be on the lookout for anything crossing over. Not likely unless they have figured out a way to navigate through the Black Wall effectively," the client said.

BB felt odd being a bystander as the deal was going down. He knew nothing of CC's clients. Where were they from? What was this thing? Why so secretive about transporting it?

"Commander Cody, permission to come aboard?" the client asked.

"Permission granted. Please leave your weapons on your ship, if you don't mind. It's an old habit of mine. I want to trust you, but you're still an unknown quantity, so I'd prefer it that way."

"We have no issue complying with your request. How shall we board?"

"I'll open one of my cargo hatches facing you. Just pull in there, wait for the green light for pressurizing, and I'll meet you there."

"Thank you, commander."

CC's leadership impressed BB. He had seen her vulnerable side and her sexual prowess had made his toes curl, but here was another side of her. In full command and ready for anything. He would not like to get into a fight with her. BB thought he would lose that scuffle. As they waited for the shuttle to arrive, CC clipped a small but powerful Zen gun on the back of her belt out of sight. Zen guns were very effective at close range. Whatever they hit disintegrated to the atomic level. Messy and kind of nasty. She was prepared for the unexpected.

The client's shuttle landed in Bay 3. Green lights lit up after the cargo hatch door was closed and the compartment pressurized. A tall thing came out of the opening of the shuttle. BB thought it looked like what he felt like every time CC tortured him with a long jump. It had long arms, long legs and a long torso. Instead of a fleshy head like a human, it had a bulb on a stem. On the front side of the bulb was a flat screen on which a human-looking face appeared. It looked very human, but you felt like you were watching an ancient black & white television set up close. The facial expression was convincing and displayed emotion as it greeted Commander Cody.

Neat trick, BB thought, but he was not sure if this was an alien creature, a robot or maybe a mixture of both with a little human tissue mixed in somewhere. The projected human-looking face made them feel comfortable. The voice was the same, so they had matched language and speech patterns to mimic humans flawlessly.

No one else came out of the shuttle, although there could be more onboard. CC, BB, and Beatrice led the way out of the bay into the hallway and down several levels to the special cargo hatch that contained CC's cargo. Once inside, the client seemed to become very excited. The smell triggered a reaction since you could not see much yet. The lights had not come on yet.

"Wonderful, Commander Cody! You have delivered our most precious prize."

The lights came on as they walked deeper into the cargo hold, and there it was, the perfect dull gray cube resting on the pedestal.

"Your friends loaded it and set it up this way. We set the humidity and temperature to their specifications. Can I ask you something?"

"Yes."

"What is that smell?"

"It's part organic, like myself. If it is healthy, it gives off a certain odor much like your sweat."

CC turned to BB and gave him a wink. BB flushed.

"It is in perfect health. We have credited your account with payment. We will return to our ship and send over a crew to remove the artifact."

BB made a mental note of the term used, "artifact."

"My crew will assist you any way we can. Thank you for your business," CC said. The TV head nodded with an expression of satisfaction. It was a happy customer.

CHAPTER SEVEN

WHERE WAS SHE RIGHT NOW? Somehow she was still aware of everything that was happening on the Merry-Go-Round. She watched through security cameras as they finished sweeping up her charred, smoking carcass. Where was BB? Zedjack, her security chief, was gone. Power struggles started to break out here and there. Who was in charge? Why was she still in the dark?

Deep inside the bowels of the Merry-Go-Round in a room camouflaged to look like a toxic gas storage room, a red light on a panel turned to green. A set of cabinet doors that ran from the ceiling down to the floor fluttered open. Sophia 2 stepped out onto the floor, blinking in the bright light.

"It worked." She had a giant smile on her face. She was an exact copy of herself in every detail. "Diagnostics, run an evaluation on Sophia 1. What caused the shutdown?" She peeked out into the hallway through a tiny crack as she opened the door ever so slowly, no one around.

In her compartment where Sophia had shut down, her still smoking body twitched ever so slightly as a techie swept up parts. He noticed it and jumped back. Weird. It was like something in her was still functioning.

Despite all the destruction, Sophia 1's documentation system was still functional because it was durable. It recorded like a black box all details of Sophia's disintegration and shutdown. Sitting several decks below, she got the data she needed. It was a sabotaged lubricant system that ruptured and ate her up. She ran a check of her own lubricant system. It was fine. Someone had contaminated Sophia 1's lubricant. It would take time to track the origin down. The list of suspects was long. She had to do her research in the data banks without drawing attention. You made enemies when you took over and ran everything. Everyone thought she was dead, so it made the hunt for the perpetrator easier since no one expected her to show back up again.

What happened to Booster Bob? She plugged into the Merry-Go-Round's newsfeed channel. Whoever did this used Booster Bob as a patsy. They made it look like he screwed up during the stimulus session and killed her. The news was full of recriminations toward him. He had escaped onto a freighter named the *Peregrine* and had disappeared. The courageous Zedjack had jumped onto the heavy cruiser, *Avenger*, and was in pursuit. That was his job, so his action was in line with his duties. He was the leader of Sophia's security team.

Was Zedjack the culprit? Sophia wondered. *I doubt it,* she thought. Playing the role of an avenging hero was a natural for him. Had this been a frontier town in the ancient Wild West, he would have been the sheriff on a white horse. If he were the one behind her assassination, he would not leave the Merry-Go-Round and let someone else take over control and ownership while he was chasing Booster Bob. Besides, Booster Bob was not responsible for her demise, although he didn't know that yet. Someone onboard the Merry-Go-Round had switched out her lubricants and had set up Booster Bob as the perpetrator. She had to figure out who it was before she could reclaim control.

Contingencies. This was one of Sophia's powerful skills. She had learned early in her existence that one cannot see the future. However, one could project it so that one can prepare for it. Thus, she created a semi-active duplicate of herself that received a perpetual update of everything Sophia thought, did, and experienced. She had also created a clandestine eavesdropping system throughout the MGR before this event. Sophia activated it now. It was composed of data bots inserted into the main Merry-Go-Round network, androids amongst the population, and a vast array of listening and surveillance systems everywhere. Sophia expected the need to do surveillance, with nobody being aware that it was going on or that she was behind it. Someone might notice the activity, but would not have any way of figuring out where it was coming from or who was behind it.

"Activate Operation 'Umbrella'," she said into her arm mounted communicator. "Search criteria: nanobots in lubricant, plots to kill Sophia, and power struggle for control of the Merry-Go-Round." These were keywords and associations that were listed, processed, and dispersed throughout Merry-Go-Round's universe. AI would decipher these commands into subsets and send out directives to all participants with specific instructions on what to look for, listen for, dig up, and observe. She encrypted it all so that the origin was impossible to determine and camouflaged so that few would notice the system was searching. The entire eavesdropping system was clandestine and protected.

Sophia was happy with herself. She had once again sustained an attack and survived. There was much to do and many questions to be answered before she reemerged and reclaimed her kingdom. Her faith in preparing for contingencies had enabled her to survive. Whoever was responsible would be very sorry they tried to murder her.

She worried about Booster Bob. Where was he? It appeared he was smart enough and fast enough to escape. For reasons unknown, the *Peregrine* made a run for it instead of turning Booster Bob over to security on the MGR. Sophia was determined to clear his name and reputation. Besides, he still owed her a session, and she wanted him and his Sparky very much. She smiled. She liked him. He treated her as an equal, and when she surprised him, he was more than delighted. Was that the beginning of a relationship?

Why would the *Peregrine*, the freighter he stowed away on, decide to make a run for it instead of returning him to MGR? Before all of this happened, she remembered scuttlebutt going around the Merry-Go-Round about someone carrying a special cargo headed for somewhere beyond the Black Wall. Could that have anything to do with it?

"Operation Umbrella: Also, give me anything you find or hear about a special cargo coming through here on its way beyond the Black Wall. Also check out the *Peregrine*." Could her cargo have something to do with why it ran? Sophia was curious.

Sophia monitored the MGR's chat channel as she worked on another backup replica of herself. It became obvious to her that Zedjack had followed the *Peregrine* to the edge of the great asteroid field, but had lost track of it. She wondered where they had gone. The chatter subsided as the search continued. Sophia focused on her work.

She was jolted out of her concentration by Zedjack's voice declaring, "As we were cruising the perimeter, a ferocious battle broke out behind us. By the time we got turned around, the *Peregrine* nailed four out of six ships that were attacking it. We determined they were a part of the Stoners Gang, space pirates well known in this area."

That must be an unusual freighter, thought Sophia. Most freighters had some defense against space pirates, but not much. This one had to be equipped with some heavy-duty hardware to pull this off. Plus, someone on board had to be a damn good shooter. Booster Bob maybe? She doubted it.

Digging into some databases, sure enough Sophia's suspicions are confirmed. It read: Freighter named *Peregrine*, commanded by Commander Cody, has been upgraded and modified with special heavy armaments for protection. She remembered meeting CC once, an indelible impression with her bright shiny spurs. Outrageous and a fighter, no one was going to steal her cargo, ever.

Sophia played her other hunch and ran a profile on BB. She knew his reputation as a highlighter, but knew nothing else about him. "Ha!" she blurted out. There it was under Other Talents: Booster Bob is an expert gamer. He won the Galactic Gaming Championship four times in a row when he was a teenager.

That explained that. *My new boyfriend is also an ace gunner. Commander Cody has aroused my curiosity,* Sophia thought. What was she carrying on that over-gunned freighter?

"Umbrella, Report No. 1: Lubricant used was verified as clean off supply ship Easterbrook III 2 cycles ago, analyzed and passed. Nanobots inserted into the lubricant in Metal Shop No. 2 just before your last lube job. End Report."

"Shit! Umbrella! Give me a list of all personnel accessing Metal Shop No. 2 during the last cycle. I want photo surveillance playback as well for the same time period." Whoever did this was going to be making a move soon to take over control of the MGR. She told herself to be patient. Her apparent death had given them a false sense of security. They would reveal themselves and make their play soon. When that happened, she would make her play as well. She waited.

"Umbrella, Report No. 2: 99.8 percent of conversations about your demise attribute it to Booster Bob. 0.2 percent take credit for it. End Report."

"Can you identify who the 0.2 percent is and where they are physically located?"

"We cannot make a positive match on the voices because they were in the audience of a floor show on the primary avenue. We can separate parts of the conversation from the background noise, but not all."

"Play it back to me."

"Noise... she's gone alright... noise... can't believe.... noise.... was so effective... noise..... noise.... take over.... noise.... tomorrow, he'll be here.... noise.... Manchester."

Sophia stiffened at the sound of that name. Manchester was an old and formidable enemy she had outplayed several times before, but she knew he never gave up. "OK, show me some visuals associated with where this conversation occurred." No one in the crowd looked familiar, but any of them could work for Manchester. "Alert security and have them notify us if Manchester shows up on this Merry-Go-Round. Don't let them know who sent the alert."

CHAPTER EIGHT

As Sophia expected, Manchester landed with his Super Fighter, the *Revenge*, within the hour. How come the security system didn't sound an alarm? Sophia watched him and his gang on security cams march up from the transportation deck to the main entrance of the Midway of the Merry-Go-Round. Beneath the spectacular dome he stopped, jacked into the sound system, and made an announcement. "Staff and customers of the Merry-Go-Round! I declare I am now the new owner and manager of this establishment."

She laughed. It was like watching an ancient explorer claim the beach for the King. Sophia reached over and turned on the mic for the audio system. "Mr. Manchester.... Whatever gave you the idea you are suddenly in charge here?"

The color drained out of Manchester's face like a bad leak in an aquarium. Her voice was so recognizable. Manchester spun around, staring at his group in vain as he swelled up like a volcano ready to blow. Sophia zoomed in on their faces. Wide-eyed surprise and a tinge of fear was obvious. Manchester stomped and screamed.

"So, Mr. Manchester, you know you are not welcome here on the Merry-Go-Round based on your behavior the last time you were here."

"Show yourself, Sophia. Are you for real, or are you just trying to fool me again?"

Sophia ran up to the second level, overlooking the main square where Manchester and his thugs stood dazed and confused. She revealed herself from behind a massive beam and waved at him like some kid at an amusement park.

Manchester went berserk, as she knew he would. He whipped up his left arm. It exploded into fire as he cut loose on her. She knew him so well. Sophia stepped behind the beam. His shots ricocheted off the beam in all directions. Patrons dove for cover. Sophia's security team expected a confrontation with someone eventually, but this was intense and dangerous. They had all been running on idle since the news of her demise, waiting to see who would take over the MGR. Once it was clear Sophia was still the boss, they opened fire on Manchester and his gang. The entire center of the Merry-Go-Round lit up with blinding flashes and deafening sound as the firefight erupted. Sophia's team had a greater number and more firepower. They were on a higher level, which provided them with a tactical advantage.

As Sophia's rain of fire started taking its toll, Manchester shouted for his gang to pull back to the ship. Several of his crew were wounded as they ran like hell, but all made it back onto the *Revenge*. As they rushed to pull away, one of Sophia's security men shot a tracker pellet that glued itself to the side of his hull. She watched Manchester pull away from the Merry-Go-Round, do a 180° turn and hit full throttle to make his getaway.

Manchester was almost seven feet tall with a massive body, and right now, Sophia imagined it quivered with rage. She was sure he was taking out his frustration on his crew. He had to be trying to figure out how in the hell she reinvented herself when he had seen video footage of her complete demise. Sophia knew he assumed framing Booster Bob was a success since Zedjack was off chasing him down somewhere out there on the *Peregrine*. Manchester was not stupid and she figured it would dawn on him that she had a backup of herself. She laughed to herself, thinking about the diatribe of cursing, screaming and whining that surely accompanied that realization. His poor crew; she felt sorry for them, but only for a second.

Sophia scrambled her two medium cruisers, the *Blade* and the *Scorpion*, to chase after Manchester. The *Revenge* was fast. She knew they couldn't catch him, but she had to make the effort just the same. The chase sent him a simple message that she would kill him on sight next time. No more pretending to be nice. He had tried to kill her with no apologies. Plus, Manchester had framed Booster Bob for the crime. He was a worthy adversary. He would return once he had recovered from his failure. Manchester never gave up. It was more than just taking over the MGR now. His hatred for robots was common knowledge. Sophia had become the focal point for him. That made her think about her options and how she would protect her second full backup once it was done. Manchester would figure that out eventually once he had time to think it through.

Manchester made a run for the asteroid fields. The *Revenge* outdistanced Sophia's light cruisers easily. Maybe he could connect with the Stoners Gang and together they could raid the Merry-Go-Round. When he arrived, he found the smoking wreckage of the Stoner ships. He also found Sophia's *Avenger* in the neighborhood snooping around. Manchester contacted it.

"This is Zedjack. What are you doing way out here, Manchester?"

"I could ask you the same question. What the hell happened here?"

"You must have heard what happened to Sophia since you came from that direction?"

Manchester could tell Zedjack was not aware that Sophia had resurrected herself since he had taken off to chase down Booster Bob. He would not tell him. "Yes, I did."

"I would have thought you would have made a move to take over the Merry-Go-Round for yourself after all the times you and Sophia have fought for control of it."

"I've got people working on that as we speak. I came out here to talk with the Stoners about going in with me on the takeover, but it looks like somebody toasted my buddies before I got here," Manchester said.

"I was pursuing Booster Bob. He killed Sophia on the MGR. He made his getaway by hopping onto Commander Cody's freighter, the *Peregrine*. I tracked them here. Commander Cody was making it difficult with her double-jumps and all. When I arrived, I think they must have been hiding inside the asteroid field because I couldn't find them."

"So what happened?"

"I'm guessing, but I'll bet the Stoners realized they were sitting next to the *Peregrine* and attacked it. Commander Cody surprised them by having way more firepower than any freighter should have, and someone on that boat knows how to shoot."

"Usually, it's the Stoners that surprise their prey. Are you saying it went the other way around this time?" Manchester tilted his head in disbelief.

"That seems to be the case... I was cruising the perimeter trying to spot them when a full-blown battle broke out behind me. By the time I got turned around, four Stoners were in flames and the *Peregrine* was gone. There was an afterglow nearby, so Commander Cody must have made a jump."

"So have you been in contact with the Merry-Go-Round?"

"No. I turned off the antennas in that direction. Not much back there that I care about. On the trip out here, I've had a lot of time to think about what to do next."

"Time for a career change, eh?" Manchester was curious about what he had on his mind. Zedjack was too conservative to join Manchester's gang, but he might not be above improving his own situation. He listened.

"Do you know anything, or have you heard anything about the cargo Commander Cody is carrying?" asked Zedjack.

"No, what have you heard?"

"Nothing specific, but she's got something onboard that freighter that is special, that's for sure."

Manchester was becoming interested as well. "Why do you say that?"

"I heard she had custom modifications made to her freighter that bordered on exotic. When that news leaked out, everybody's imaginations went into overdrive. Plus, why would she protect Booster Bob if he killed Sophia? It doesn't make sense."

"What do you think it is?"

"I don't know, but I know a bunch of people are trying to find out. She would not be running this hard unless she doesn't want anybody snooping around on the *Peregrine*. So while I'm chasing Booster Bob for killing Sophia, I might also pursue a cargo that could be valuable."

CHAPTER NINE

CC's CLIENT signaled to its craft sitting on the floor of the cavernous transportation deck. A large door on the craft slid open and a crew of strange four-foot-high beings waddled out onto the floor and moved toward the cargo compartment. They surrounded the cube, making hoots, hollers, and squeaks like little kids when they think they've found something free, like ice cream. The air was electric with sounds of jubilation.

"May I ask you a question now that you are taking possession of your cargo?"

"Of course, Commander Cody."

"What exactly is it? I understand it is partly organic, thus the smell, but what is its purpose and how does it function?"

"I am not surprised you want to know what this object you have transported to us is. As Aggregators, we collect far and wide throughout the universe. Most of our collection is stable. We are not clear what this is or how it functions. Those that live in the area where we found it have warned us. It can be quite violent if provoked. In some far parts of the universe, these seed pods are revered as gods."

"So this thing could go berserk on us or you, if provoked?" CC said.

"Yes, it is alive, therefore unpredictable. Let's start with the smell. Just like your organic foods and your physical bodies, if they are past their ripeness, then they smell, start to decay and eventually rot," the client said. "Organic emotion is one of the strongest forces in the universe. We are trying to work out a way to harness this power in new ways that perpetuate growth and stop the breakdown of physical structure."

"Are you working on a mechanism that will eliminate the effects of aging, time, and deterioration?" BB jumped right in since he was an expert at judging and using the hookup between emotions and nervous systems in humans, aliens, robots and cyborgs.

CC introduced BB. "This is Booster Bob, who is catching a ride with us."

The client straightened up in stature, like he remembered he was slouching a little in reaction to what CC had said. There was an awkward delay, silence. Then he said, "You are 'the famous Booster Bob'? The man who made our Queen smile?"

CC shook her head and mumbled something to herself about BB being a god damned "rock star" stowaway.

BB smiled. "Yes, I am Booster Bob.. You must be talking about Queen Xnar on the planet of Creosote?"

"I am." The client smiled brightly. "That day so long ago, you brought a moment of euphoria to our great Queen. She still talks about it today. It changed her forever. You are so much more than a highlighter."

"Well, I'd like to think so, but who am I to say? I provide a service to all, and in return, they reward me. It's a good living, or it was until now."

"How so?" the client said.

"I was giving Sophia, the Merry-Go-Round owner and manager, a session when she disintegrated on me. Someone set me up, but I didn't know it. Everybody there naturally thinks I fucked up and killed her, so I had to run for it. Thus here I am, a stowaway on Commander Cody's *Peregrine*."

"That is unfortunate. I am sorry you are being hunted for something that you did not do. Eventually, the truth will come out and you will once again be able to bring happiness to all."

"I hope you are right," BB said. "So tell me more about what this seed of yours is about."

"A very long time ago, we Aggregators sent out surveyor ships in all directions to search the universe, to document it and bring back what seemed significant. Those ships returned after a very long time, overloaded with curiosities from thousands of solar systems. We inventoried it all and created a unique compilation of life's secrets, such as emotions, intelligence, love, hate, aggression, and more."

CC said, "So you knew what you were doing and just built an immense collection or museum?"

"Yes, but we made mistakes here and there as we built out the aggregate. A catastrophe here and there, but overall, we have been able to handle most items effectively."

"So while this is stable now, it could become unstable because it is alive?" BB asked.

"It has been stable since we collected it, but we received it under extreme conditions from its mother."

"From its mother... Can you describe its mother? What does the seed do when it is unstable?" CC asked as she noticed her body temperature jump and she started sweating.

"We're not sure, but its mother is a giant monster plant type of thing that has developed an incredible array of weapons. If it thinks it is in danger, it will defend itself. We have had incidents when it misread our intentions and it surprised us."

"That's a nice way of saying it," BB said. "I'm not sure I want to hear details of that episode."

"We convinced it of its error and it was very embarrassed and sad. It was a learning experience on both sides. Few know about its existence. Those that know something about it or have heard rumors have decided it is valuable beyond comparison to anything else."

"So everybody wants to own it," CC said.

"Yes, I am afraid so. What they do not realize is that they cannot possess it for personal profit. It knows everything and has intelligence that far exceeds anything known to us. So far, it has been humble about its capabilities and has not shown hostility or arrogance. We think this is a wonderful development."

"If it was a bad boy, could you stop it?" CC asked.

"We do not know. This is a creation of the universe that we have discovered through our exploration and feeble knowledge. Part of the reason that we are out this far from all other activity is to isolate it. We're not expecting anything to go wrong, but there is evil in the universe," the client said.

BB and CC looked at each other as if they could read each other's mind. *Do these Aggregators have any clue what they are doing? Nope.*

"Listen, if you need any help, we'd be glad to assist you. I'm still curious what makes this thing tick and what is it capable of doing?" BB said.

The client's screen head showed a face distorted in consideration. An awkward silence fell upon them. Then it spoke. "There are some issues we could use some help on if you are genuine in your interest."

"Of course I am." BB looked at CC with his eyebrows raised, as if trying to communicate with her telepathically again. "Let me come with you over to your ship and you can show me this thing and maybe give me a little demonstration."

"That would be fine," the customer said.

"Let me confer with Commander Cody here for a second before I join you. Go ahead. I'll catch up to you."

The client nodded.. He turned and walked toward his craft. CC walked over to BB and leaned toward him so they could speak in lower voices. "CC, I don't know what I'm getting myself into here, but I just have an uneasy feeling about this thing."

"I'm terrified these clowns have collected something that could turn nasty and unstable. I admire their curiosity, but their methods have not always been successful," CC whispered.

"Good. So we're both reading this the same way," BB said. "It's a hodgepodge that is not integrated, so parts of it could go off the rails and bring the whole thing down. Normally, I couldn't care less, but your client has also collected a variety of weaponry from across time and the entire universe. I have no plan, but I'll be back soon, I hope."

"You had better be back, BB. You still owe me, remember?"

"Oh my, I think that's a date, right?"

"Right. Stay in contact. Let me know what the hell is going on. Also, we don't want to hang around this neighborhood too long in case anyone is following us."

"OK." BB saluted her. Why did he keep doing that?

CC looked at him with a blank face. What the hell is he doing? She returned the salute. It was strange behavior for both of them. Were they trying to convince the aliens they were old military comrades?

CHAPTER TEN

BB CAUGHT up with the client as he walked up the ramp into his craft. The door on the craft closed, and it moved out of *Peregrine*'s transportation deck and headed back to the *Golden Globe*. He looked back at the *Peregrine* and realized it felt like leaving home somehow. In such a short time, he had grown attached to CC, Beatrice, and #1 & #2.

As the client shuttlecraft approached the *Golden Globe*, BB could see more detail of its surface. It did not look like metal. It radiated light from inside through what looked like some type of plastic or translucent gel. A round hole diaphragm opened, and the craft slid through it. Inside, the light was brilliant as well. These beings liked lots of light. Maybe they fed off it. BB knew from experience that this meant they came from a planet or place that was close to bright stars. Other creatures of the universe came from dark and cold planets long distances from warm, bright stars. They enjoyed living in the shadows.

BB walked out into the landing area with his host. More small beings rushed up and greeted them and those on the shuttle. These were three feet tall and looked like a reddish cloth draped over a low bush. He could not see any appendages, and yet they glided around in smooth arcs. As a group, they swarmed onto the shuttle. Out floated the ominous flat black box, and it seemed like they were controlling it somehow with an unseen magnetic field. It settled to the surface while all admired it.

"Let me show you what it looks like inside," the client said. They walked over to a corner near the back of the area. The walls came alive with enormous monitors floor to ceiling, and out in front of this wall was an animated three-dimensional display that came alive as well.

"Marvelous… fascinating," was the best that BB could manage. A blend of beauty, danger, and total chaos was what it was. The flat black box unfolded in front of them with no one touching it. It revealed a gigantic seed pod about two feet long and one foot across. Energy was shooting out of it in all directions, some making connections with other nodes, many just going off into space at random. Its surface looked organic, with a brown color and rough surface, but it glowed and shimmered with sparks here and there. A cloud of heavy dust undulated around it. "Will you allow me to record some of this so I can take it back to the *Peregrine* and show it to Commander Cody?"

"I see no reason not," the client said. He stepped out of the way. BB recorded the total scene in two and three dimensions.

"Tell us what you think after you have had time to analyze it. We are concerned with the instability it manifests from time to time. We have tried to integrate it, but it resists," the client said.

BB said. "I'd be happy to look at it, and I'm sure Commander Cody would as well."

"Booster Bob, your system stimulator and highlighter skills could give us a different, more effective perspective."

"I'll try to see if I can make any sense out of it. No guarantees, but I am intrigued by its inherent beauty and complexity, like a mini-universe in a seed," BB said.

"Good. Go back to the *Peregrine* and determine if you can help us. Here are some other oddities we have found over the years. Please share these with Commander Cody. I'm sure she'll enjoy them." BB hopped into a space scooter, a small transportation device for short distances, and returned to the *Peregrine*.

"Welcome back, cowboy. How did it go over there?" CC asked.

Shaking his head from side to side, he said, "They have built a unique chaotic mini-universe in part of their ship. When the black box opened up and revealed the seed pod, it seems like other artifacts reacted to its presence in a disturbing way. It is just plain scary. There are also hundreds of exotic weapons stored in the same compartment. There seems to be no evidence of an overall control system."

"That doesn't sound good. Why did they do this and what is the purpose... the Aggregators?"

"Well, they don't have a suitable answer. My first response was to tell them to take all of this stuff and put it back where they found it. It is like messing with the general design of the universe's plan or something equivalent. That's my conservative side, then my wild boy side gets all excited because of the unknown potential of such a contraption. It could tap into millions of civilizations."

"And it also could lead other life forms back here that are not nice. The weapons scare me the most," CC grimaced. "No wonder others want it. It means power if they get it and control it, but that is a big if."

"They seem concerned, but not quite capable of comprehending the dangerous aspect of their collection. Like kids playing with a stick of explosives," BB said. "Let me show you the images of it and see what you think."

BB ran through all his still images of the massive wall monitors and the video clip of the animated three-dimensional display. CC was impressed. She had more questions than BB could answer.

"I'm a systems kind of guy. I know how humans, robots, aliens and cyborgs work, how their life support systems function and work together. That allows me to hack their systems and give them pleasant sensations that they are incapable of creating for themselves. This is different," he said.

"There is no organization system or structure here as far as I can see," CC said. "It's like they have collected things from all over the universe and thrown them into a box. They want everything to play nice with each other, but it is not working together at all, which creates instability," CC said.

"Exactly. Somehow, they expect me to come up with a remedy. If I was even going to try, I would not know where to start. Is Sparky capable of imposing an operating system into this chaos? Would the seed pod respond or try to eliminate the irritant?"

"Good luck with that, Booster Bob," CC said. "Let me know if there is any way I can help. Meanwhile, I am going to do some maintenance on *Peregrine* so we can get out of here when the time comes."

"Yeah, that makes sense. Can I borrow Beatrice for a while? She could help me analyze this thing, plus they gave me some other things to look at and analyze as well."

"Yes. She can help you. Where are you going to do your analysis?" CC asked.

"I think we'll set up in the sick bay of the *Peregrine* since most of the hardware is there, and if I'm going to build something and program it, that would be the logical place to do it."

"OK. Do you think you can help them out?"

"To be honest, I don't know. Finding a seashell on the beach is not the same as discovering how that seashell lived when it was alive. It is a relic, an artifact, but it is also alive, not dead, so that changes everything. That means if I am going to be successful, I am going to have to guess a lot. I have a good imagination, but I don't know if it will be enough. We'll see."

"We can hang around here for a while. See what you can come up with. I'd offer suggestions, but this is beyond me."

"Yeah, me too, really, but I'll try it. See you later," BB said.

"Holler if you need anything."

"Thanks." BB grabbed Sparky along with assorted stuff and headed downstairs along with Beatrice to the sick bay. He used the counter top to display his stills and video on analysis monitors, which allowed him to zoom in on any detail. Beatrice helped keep a record of everything he discovered as he went along. After several hours of looking hard at everything he could see, he stopped and pushed himself back away from the counter and reclined in his chair. He was tired, and before he knew it, he slipped off into a nap. BB regularly used this technique for creative incubation. He wanted to understand the chaos and create order in the fishbowl. As he went to sleep, Beatrice slipped out to get BB some food from the galley.

Beatrice walked into the sick bay with food for BB. Her arrival woke him up, which was fine because he had napped at least a half-hour to forty-five minutes, and that was enough.

"Thank you, Beatrice. I'm starving."

"You are welcome, BB. So what do you think so far?"

"Nothing much yet, but I am optimistic. I am trying to figure out some way for Sparky to integrate with this energetic seed pod. I may have to build a new spark box that comes at this challenge from a whole new direction."

"Is that possible?" Beatrice said.

"I don't know, but I can't come up with any other solution. So that's what I am going to do. I want you to document every new circuit or configuration I build. OK, let's get started."

"I am curious about the origins of your spark box, Sparky. How did you invent it?" Beatrice asked.

"I didn't invent it. Its origin comes from ancient times on Earth, from a country called Mexico. It was called a shock box, or toques! It delivered a shock, and they used it for entertainment. People would pay money/credits to be shocked and to see who in a group could stand the strongest shock for fun."

"That does not sound like fun."

"I agree, but remember, those were ancient times. Fun was different back then. I found a diagram showing how to construct a shock box, so I built one and tried it. It shocked me... literally."

"Brilliant," Beatrice said.

"Ha! Yes, I agree. I wanted to experience it directly instead of reading about it. That's when I came up with the idea of a changed shock box that could create pleasure rather than pain."

"I can attest to your success. I have experienced nothing else in my existence that felt that good," she said, smiling.

"Thank you, Beatrice. I am honored with your gratitude. Now let's see if we can build a spark box that will control that thing."

CHAPTER ELEVEN

ZEDJACK WONDERED what was happening right now back on the Merry-Go-Round. Power struggles for control would erupt soon unless he apprehended Booster Bob and brought him back for justice. Zedjack would assert his position as the new Manager based on his rank, privilege and firepower. Was that what he wanted to do?

Manchester's goal to take over the Merry-Go-Round was general knowledge. Zedjack had fought him before with Sophia several times and they had prevailed so far. Even though it looked like Booster Bob had taken out Sophia, he didn't quite buy the whole thing. What if Manchester somehow set up Booster Bob to make it look like he had murdered her? It would not be a surprise to find out Manchester was somehow involved, but he didn't know how.

Zedjack realized, pausing in his conversation with Manchester, he was being pretty stupid telling him rumors about valuable cargo being on the *Peregrine. Why would I tell him about a secret cargo?* He was a murderer, a conman, a first-class scoundrel. Zedjack was getting an odd feeling. The hairs on the back of his neck stiffened. *What the hell is Manchester really doing out here if Sophia is dead? Why hadn't he already taken over the Merry-Go-Round?* He didn't need the Stoners to help him. Something did not smell right. Zedjack turned off the communication mic and barked an order to his communications offi-cer. "Contact the Merry-Go-Round and see who is in charge there right now."

"Will do, sir," the com officer said.

"Quietly, I want the shields deployed so Manchester doesn't know they are up and running. Gunners, eyes wide open now. Be ready for anything," Zedjack commanded.

"Sir, Sophia wants to talk to you," the com officer said. The man's lower jaw hung open like a broken hinge, like he had just talked with a ghost.

Zedjack rotated around in a slow motion swing as if he was dancing in a ballet. "What did you say?"

"Sophia is happy you re-opened communications with her," the com officer answered.

"Make sure our link to Manchester is on hold and muted," Zedjack switched to Sophia's channel. "Sophia! Is that really you?"

"Yes. It is me, Zed. I've returned from the dead."

"How did you do that?"

"Backup duplicate linked to me so that if anything happened, it would fully activate and come to life. Yeah, I know. It must seem bizarre from your perspective."

"So I am staring at Manchester a couple of miles away. We are on the edge of the asteroid field. I have my shields up. What should I expect from him?"

"The worst. He tried to take over the Merry-Go-Round. It was he who made it look like Booster Bob had killed me. It had nothing to do with BB. Manchester contaminated my lubricants, so that when the session started, it triggered their corrosive nano-bot attack."

A sound like a muffled thud flooded Zedjack's control deck and rocked the cruiser. "Whoa! Manchester probably figured out I'm talking to you. Back to you later, Sophia. I need to engage him before he blows my shields away. Signing off."

Zedjack didn't need to give the order to fire back. His gunners fired a synchronized volley at Manchester's ship. Lasers and missiles bounced off each ship's shields, creating a spectacular light show. The duel turned into a barrage of terrible fire power being thrown back and forth by both ships. Zedjack's *Avenger* was bigger and stronger and could sustain its defensive shields. It had plenty of firepower, but no special advantage against Manchester's souped-up *Revenge*. Manchester had strong firepower, including some unique weapons, but he couldn't last in a shield standoff battle.

Without warning, Manchester made a jump and disappeared, leaving nothing behind, or so it seemed.

"Shit! He's made a jump. Check the vector for his departure. He is trying to make a getaway," Zedjack said.

"Sir, he went straight into the Black Wall. We could set up a series of sequential jumps and see if we can catch up to him."

"Alright, let's try that. I hate to lose." The *Avenger* shook with a savage sideways jolt. Everyone on the bridge flew across the room piling up at the bottom of the opposite wall. The deafening sound of an explosion and rushing air flooded the room. Multiple alarms went off, causing a massive wall of light and sound. Automatic life support defense strategies kicked in, shutting off sections that had lost their integrity. Fire extinguishers turned on where needed. Zedjack was still conscious, but dazed and confused as he pulled himself up and off a pile of his fellow crew members.

"Damage report!" he yelled, coughing from the dust and smoke that filled the bridge.

His crew was trying to stand back up. Some could not get up to help. Those that could function gradually started assessing what still worked and what did not. Whatever hit them had done major damage. An entire section of their port side was no longer there. It would take some time to stabilize systems, help the wounded, and see if the primary engine would still work.

"What the hell was that? And how did that happen after Manchester was gone?" Zedjack screamed.

His first officer responded, "I think it was a 'LBB,' sir, a leave-behind bomb. They have their own cloaking device so you can't detect them. It links onto us and waits for us to lower our shields and then, BANG! It detonates."

"Why didn't I know about these damned things?"

"Because they are rare, expensive and glitchy. If the bad guy doesn't leave fast enough, it can target him."

"Fuck! Well, guess we won't be chasing Manchester or anybody else. Contact Sophia and give her the great news. We are still alive, but we have major damage and have lost crew members. We may have to be rescued. I am going down to the propulsion deck and see if our engine is still intact. Keep me posted."

CHAPTER TWELVE

Booster Bob had looked over almost all the things that he had hauled back from the *Golden Globe*. Most of it was curious and odd. There was one box he had not opened yet, so he dragged it over to the foot of the main table and lifted it up onto it. The lid came off easily. "That's weird," BB said.

"What's weird? All this stuff is strange to me," Beatrice said.

"This looks like something round inside of a carrying case. I've seen this kind of thing in ancient images from Earth. It was a sport. I think it was called 'bowling' and this looks like a bowling ball bag." He pulled the bag out of the box, using the handle built into the top of the bag. He unzipped the top and looked inside. "What the hell?"

"Booster Bob... use language to explain what you are seeing, please," Beatrice said. She displayed her exasperation by putting her hands on her hips while leaning forward, tapping one foot.

"Sorry. It also looks like a crystal ball. That, too, is an ancient mystical concept from Earth. A crystal ball was a fortune-telling object associated with clairvoyance and seeing into the future."

"Fascinating," Beatrice said. "Pull it out. Let's have a look at it in the light."

BB grasped the round ball with both hands and pulled it up. The finger and thumb holes were missing, and it felt cold, like glass. When he lifted it onto the table, it generated a dim flicker. It changed colors and flickered again. It became illuminated from within, lit up. A smell of hot metal became apparent as a thin wisp of smoke came out of the top. It was acting like it was booting up or turning on somehow.

BB and Beatrice stared at the ball. It was generating its own weather system inside the ball. It snapped clear... everything in the sickbay showed up inside the ball like a reflection.

Reaching to touch it once more, BB tracked his own reflection as his arm attached to his hand stretched out. On contact, a voice came out of the crystal ball. "Wait a minute. There is someone on the other side," it said. The voice sounded just like Booster Bob's.

Beatrice and BB turned their heads toward each other with eyes wide-open and mouths agape. "You just heard that, right, Beatrice?" BB said.

"I heard you," the voice in the crystal ball said. BB leaned in close to the ball's mercurial surface. So did BB inside the ball. "I see you too," it said.

"Are you recording this, Beatrice?"

"Oh yes, indeed."

"So, what is going on here? Who are you and why do you look exactly like me? Well, almost exactly like me?" BB asked with a tremble in his voice.

"My name is Bruster Bill and I am a mood adjuster. Who are you?" it said.

"I am Booster Bob and I do something similar, I think. What are we both experiencing here?"

Bruster Bill shook his head in slow motion wonderment and said, "I do not know. We've had this crystal ball around here for years and it did nothing."

"It could be a parallel universe window. I found this magic sphere in a client's vehicle who had been collecting artifacts from all over the universe. They found it somewhere and brought it back. I've been trying to figure out what it is and how it works and then you appeared," Booster Bob said.

"Beatrice, get CC down here. She needs to see this," BB said. Beatrice leaned over BB's shoulder to peek into the crystal ball, and just as she did, her duplicate on the other side did the same. They both jumped back in unison and let out a high-pitched yelp. Beatrice ran from the compartment. BB felt like he needed to explain Beatrice to Bruster, but then he realized he had an assistant just like Beatrice.

"So, Bruster, that must be your assistant as well, right?"

"Yes. She is my helper. Her name is Betty."

BB's mind was in hyper-drive mode. Everyone had heard of parallel universes, but there was no proof. What to do about it? Maybe nothing.

"I know this is going to sound odd, but what do you think we should do about this? I mean, I'm not sure if this kind of thing is common on your side or not, but it has not happened before on my side."

Bruster Bill nodded his head in agreement. "It's the same here. It has always been there in the background, almost like folklore, but no one ever found such a thing. I need to have my ship's commander see this. She is on her way down here now."

"Same here," BB said.

CC walked into the compartment with her right eyebrow arched up, causing wrinkles on her forehead. "What's the story, BB? Beatrice was hysterical, trying to explain what you've discovered."

BB said it looked like a link to a parallel universe through a bowling ball in a bowling ball bag.

"What the hell is a bowling ball?"

"Oh. It's an ancient sport played back in old times on the planet Earth. Groups of people would organize themselves into tribes, or I think they called them teams, and they would compete to see who could knock down the most pins."

"Pins?" CC asked.

"Originally, they were wooden objects that were about this high."

BB gestured with both hands, showing the approximate height. "They were larger at the bottom than the top and weighed about three and a half pounds. Each person got two turns to knock ten pins down with a bowling ball. They would roll the ball down a narrow alley made of wood. They would set the pins up at the end of the alley in a triangle-shaped arrangement."

"OK... OK. Enough. It sounds almost as bad as that other game you explained to me where you hit a white ball all over the countryside and then run after it and hit again until you find a little hole to shoot it into... Just stop, show me this thing."

Booster Bob walked over to the bowling ball bag sitting on the table. In a grand gesture with his arms, he pointed to the glassy ball resting next to the bag. "Tah! Dah!"

BB could tell Commander Cody was hesitant from a distance. He watched her forcing herself to walk up to it, lean over and stare into the round thing and there, staring back at her, was herself. She yelped and jumped back away from the bowling ball. So did the other person inside the ball. BB stepped forward.

"Let me make introductions if I may...." BB said as he gestured toward CC. "This is Commander Cody, she is the Captain of the *Peregrine*. And your name is...?"

"My name is Commander Lodi and I run the *Vinny*." Both women came back to the bowling ball and looked each other over more closely. BB could not believe his eyes. CC seemed to have forgot her fear as she just stared at the other woman. He had to admit she was attractive. Lodi wore something that looked like metal fabric, like feathers almost, but not. It reflected light and shimmered at the same time.

"How do you get that effect with your eye makeup?" CC asked without a flinch.

"Oh... well, it's called chameleon, and it's interactive, depending on your mood and light level," Commander Lodi said. "It makes my eyes look like they are open even when they are not."

"Outstanding," CC said. "I really like your outfit too. Mine is so.... filthy and drab."

BB rolled his eyes when he noticed that Bruster Bill was doing the same thing and he laughed despite himself. Both women were gorgeous from his point of view. Their outfits were skin tight, but one looked like a flying metallic eagle and the other looked like a greasy mechanic. While they seemed related in terms of their positions—both were commanders—their style could not be more different and each looked at the other with great interest.

CHAPTER THIRTEEN

MANCHESTER'S last attempt was successful. If Sophia had not constructed a backup duplicate of herself, he would be in charge of the Merry-Go-Round right now. Her body shuddered like she was experiencing a chill, which was impossible. It was a mental chill that ran up and down her metal spine. The full impact of how close she had come to being eliminated arrived in her deepest parts. "He must have been stunned to see me show up again... the bastard!" she said out loud.

Having retreated from the battle scene for the time being, Sophia continued working on her top priority now, which was completing another backup duplicate of herself in her hidden workshop deep within the MGR's guts. She was not taking any chances since her fail-safe plan had worked so well for her during this last attack by Manchester. Sophia felt sad about Booster Bob taking the rap and being framed by Manchester. Customers on the Merry-Go-Round were still trying to figure out who did what to whom and why, but they didn't really care as long as they could go back to their drinks, food, and entertainment.

For a guy like Booster Bob, losing your reputation was the worst thing that could happen to you. His reputation preceded him wherever he traveled. It took many years to establish that recognition and trust. Humans, robots, and the mixes (cyborgs) plus other species all sang praises of his work. He was well liked. BB could make you laugh even when you were feeling bad. Sophia decided she would clear up the whole mess later. Maybe she would do a sector-wide interview that explained all the details about the event and clear his name. She recalled her last moments of consciousness before the blackness descended upon her. The look on BB's face was so sad, contorted, mad, and confused when it all happened. Sophia knew at that moment it was not his fault and she told him so before dying.

Finished. Sophia carefully maneuvered her double into what looked like a huge air duct tube. She activated her link to it, triggered the security schemes, and then sealed up the tube. It all looked like part of the life support system, and most of it was, except for the hiding place.

She returned upstairs to continue repair work of damage she and Manchester had caused during their brief but fierce fire fight. The rest of her crew focused on handing out free stuff to her shaken customers, who were in shock after being caught in the middle of the fight. There is nothing that will kill a vacation buzz quicker than a near death experience. They turned the music up louder while complimentary drinks, food and discounts were given out to the wide-eyed mob. They even introduced a subtle tranquilizer into the ventilation system to calm down the clients. Nothing illegal, just a little something to brighten up the situation, a mood shifter. Crowd noise dissipated back into laughter and fun as they returned to the games and entertainment filled stages along the Midway. Sophia smiled. Her empire was still intact and functioning.

The rescue/retrieval ship, the *Saint Bernard*, had left to bring back Zedjack and his crew. They would decide at the location whether the *Avenger* was worth towing back for repair. Sophia's synthetic forehead wrinkled. Manchester's path of destruction was adding up to significant losses. She was going to have to kill him if she ever wanted any peace. He had come damn close to ending her this time using Booster

Bob as a patsy. If she hadn't backed herself up, she would not be here. Again, her body involuntarily shivered at the thought.

"Zedjack. Which way do you think Manchester went when he bugged out?" Sophia said.

"Good question…. We tried to get a tracer on the *Revenge*'s hull before the shooting started. Don't know if my attempt was successful or not."

"Understood. We may have tagged him as he made his getaway from the MGR. Try our access codes and see if there's any info. It would be nice to know which direction he went. *Saint Bernard* is on its way. How bad are things there?"

"Bad… we have been able to stabilize the ship. Life support is back in operation. I'm afraid our engines are useless. I have many people wounded and several dead. That's my fault. Should have expected the leave-behind bomb."

"Hey! Don't be hard on yourself. You were after who you thought was the culprit and it turned out to be Manchester instead of Booster Bob. He almost got me this time. I didn't see that coming either, and I should have. After we all recover, we need to take his ass out permanently."

"I couldn't agree more. I'll get back to you as soon as I can on his vector information, if it's available."

Sophia turned off the com link. She admired Zedjack's initiative, his willingness to lay down his life for her, but she was not naïve. In this part of the galaxy, you had to be alert to everything around you. It was not like a predatory trap; it was just that everybody was looking for a way to survive and if that meant violence or betrayal, then so be it. Law was a relative thing. Living on the edge of a frontier was both exhilarating and dangerous. You could not be more free or vulnerable at the same time. Sophia suspected Zedjack chased the *Peregrine* for more than one reason. Who could blame him for thinking that his job at the Merry-Go-Round was over because of her death?

Where were Booster Bob and the *Peregrine*? They had propelled themselves into the Black Wall at the edge of the boundary, like they knew where they were going. Commander Cody had a cargo to deliver and her client, who lived on the other side. It wasn't like no one had ever gone beyond the Black Wall, but the fact was that few returned. That could mean they all found something better on the other side or that whomever or whatever lived on the other side had devoured them. Sophia always felt those fairy tales were baseless and intended to keep others out. It was like the ancient frontier days, where people were unwilling to leave the known world because of the unknown. It was a common ploy used on all frontiers. Keep it scary and dangerous and folks will avoid it.

The few that returned had some wild tales to tell, however. Many spoke of gigantic creatures similar to deep sea predators back on Earth when it had oceans. The stories all ended the same. The monsters ate the intruders.

Sophia wanted to contact Booster Bob, but lacked the information to do so. She could wait. BB could take care of himself. Besides Booster Bob, what was the *Peregrine* carrying that required it to be delivered on the other side? Had to be valuable or powerful, maybe both. She planned to discuss joining the treasure hunt with Zedjack. He came back online with directions. The tracer they had tagged him with when he left the Merry-Go-Round was active and gave the exact direction.

She realized Manchester was after the same prize most likely, especially since he failed at his coup attempt on the Merry-Go-Round. Predators like that have to keep feeding off the system or they don't survive. He had picked up enough info from Zedjack to make him curious... curious enough to cross the Black Wall and track down the *Peregrine*? Maybe she should go after him after all. It would be an opportunity to rid herself of Manchester and maybe find some treasure too. After all that, then she would collect what Booster Bob still owed her, a full pleasure session. She smiled to herself.

"Sophia." The voice of her PR director brought her back to reality. "Repairs are complete and the customers are happy with your offers to refund and receive bonus credits. They are back in line for a Merry-Go-Round ride."

"Glad to hear that. Nice work. Tell your crew it's appreciated and that I will reward them. It's almost like it never happened." She cursed Manchester in her head. That bastard cost her a bundle of credits and he damn near got away with killing her. *It's my turn. Batter up.*

CHAPTER FOURTEEN

"Just step back from it, CC," Booster Bob said. "I don't think it is what it seems."

CC stopped her conversation with her other self in mid-sentence. "What do you mean?"

"I'm saying there's something weird going on here and I don't think it's a parallel universe." Howls of disagreement exploded from the bowling ball in unison. "Just put it back into the bag and zip it closed. Let me contact your client to see if he knows anything more about this before we go any further. If they confirm it's a parallel universe link, then we can continue. If not, then we should know what we're dealing with here."

CC's face shriveled into a prune. BB knew she was not happy about cutting off her conversation with herself. He watched her glance at Beatrice, who gave her an imperceptible nod. "Fine!" She zipped up the bowling bag as the occupants continued to howl in protest.

BB wondered what Beatrice knew that neither of them understood. It was like she was saying... *Yeah, you better stop. This is not what it appears to be.* BB shook his head, trying to clear the fog. "Let's contact your client."

He thought it felt a little bit like a scam. Are things as they seem or not?

CC shook her head like she was shaking off some kind of spell. "What just happened? I want to talk to her some more. I have so many questions, but I feel mesmerized too. What the hell is going on here?"

"Exactly my feeling. I don't know what this is or how it is interacting with us, but it feels addictive," BB said.

"Beatrice, patch me through to our client," CC said.

Seconds later, the client's head appeared on the scene. CC gestured for BB to ask his questions.

"How can I help you?"

"Well, yes, I hope you can. One artifact you sent over, along with others, for CC and me to analyze is a glass-like ball in a bag with a zipper on it. When we examined it, we discovered what we think is a parallel universe link. We see ourselves in another place and we can communicate with them directly, but something is not right. Do you know anything more about this object?" BB asked.

The client began to shake and make strange, eerie sounds. It bent over in what was a death throe or hysterics.

"Is it laughing or dying?" BB asked.

"I don't know what it's doing. I'm feeling foolish, but I don't know why," CC said.

It stopped convulsing and fought to regain composure. "I'm sorry for my reaction," the client said. "We call it a sympathetic mirror.... "

CC and BB stared at each other. "You mean it's a mirror, not a link to a parallel universe?" BB said.

"Precisely. It mirrors the person looking at it and all the surroundings as well. But beyond that, it psychologically analyzes the viewer and enhances the reflection to satisfy the hopes and dreams of that person."

"That explains a lot." CC dropped her head down as she mumbled, "She is such a hot version of me." She deflated in slow motion.

"CC! You are the hottest, most filthy, stinking commander I've ever seen and I love it when you drool," BB said. He realized he maybe was sharing too much, could have maybe used better adjectives and perhaps not be so graphic, but hell. OK, so he, too, got turned on by women who smelled tired. So what?

CC brightened a little. "I may take some time to process that compliment."

"I mean, you are fine the way you are," BB said.

"That sounds boring again... go back to the filthy, smelly part..."

"It is an addictive thing," the client said. "Half organic, half machine, it tries to imitate people. It can sometimes accurately guess a person's personality, dreams, and fantasies."

"You say it's addictive... how so?" BB said.

"Entities like their other selves more than they like their real selves. After a while, they become so attached to their better selves, they become co-dependent."

"Her eye makeup is better than mine, not that it bothers me... much," BB heard CC grumble to herself.

"So most of the stuff you gave me to bring over to the *Peregrine* is interesting, especially this bowling ball. Are there other things you have collected that you find puzzling or even threatening?" BB said.

"Yes, there is... it is the item that Commander Cody delivered to us. We know it is a seed, but we think it might be much more than that, so before we shipped it from the other side of the universe, we put it inside an impregnable container."

"OK. So what's the problem?" BB said.

"We unpacked the seed. You saw it when you visited us. After you left, it became more active, maybe even irritated."

"Tell me again how you found the seed to begin with?" CC said.

"We came upon a massive living organic being in the middle of nowhere that had long arms, branches and leaves. Its defense system was too destructive, so we left it alone. As we turned to leave, the thing started launching seed pods at us. Like it wanted us to take one of its seeds, like a weed in a field and, sure enough, one of the seed pods stuck to the hull of our ship."

BB felt a rash of dread creep up his body from his gut. He recognized this reliable instinct of his, which had saved him so many times before. Call it a red flag, a flashing light, whatever.... it was telling him that this was a dangerous thing they had brought back with them. "Where is this seed now?" BB asked.

"We moved it into a shielded compartment and we are monitoring it. It is radioactive, and it changes colors and it puts off a much stronger smell than before... it's getting bigger. There has been no sign of a sprout yet, but we fear it might germinate."

"Great," BB said. "That's all we need... a growing radioactive seed that changes colors and stinks and is maybe on the brink of germinating. None of those characteristics are attractive."

"We don't expect you to solve the riddle, but we would appreciate your perspective. To be honest, we are not confident our analysis is correct. We experience a sense of danger, even foreboding, when we are close to it."

"I have the same feeling and I saw it when it was in a relatively calm state."

"Would you like to see it again and help perhaps?"

With a sigh of resignation, BB said, "Of course I'd like to help out if I can."

"We will send a shuttle craft over to pick you up, plus all the other objects you have been studying for us."

"I'd like to keep the globe a while longer," CC said.

"Fine with us. Be careful." The screen went dark.

BB and CC looked at each other. "Should we back out of all this? I know we've offered to help, but I feel like we're getting into something that may be way beyond our capabilities," CC said.

BB nodded in agreement.

"Let me look at it again and try to hook up Sparky to it. I will keep you informed on what's happening, so in case it turns to shit, I can make a run for it. Is that OK?"

"Sure, that's fine with me. Why do I feel so creepy about all this?"

"Because it seems to be getting worse. Have you noticed how we assume these people know what they're doing? These cosmic Aggregators have brought back something from the far reaches of the cosmos that is a huge chunk of the unknown. Evil? Good? Dangerous? Nobody knows yet. What could go wrong? Everything!" As he walked toward the loading bay where the shuttle craft would arrive, he said he would be back. "I'll leave my communicator turned on so you can at least hear everything that's going on. I'm taking Sparky as well."

"Take care of yourself. If it gets crazy, run for it... you're good at that," CC said.

"Hilarious, smarty pants. You're drooling again," BB retorted.

"Ready for another dance, eh, partner? Listen, I'm serious. I'll have the *Peregrine* on standby in case we need to get out of here in a hurry."

"Good idea." He smiled at her.

"I'm ready to drool with you anytime, BB. Don't get yourself hurt," CC said.

They both laughed. He saluted her again, and she returned it. *What the hell?* BB headed for the shuttle bay. His taxi was waiting. Off he went, back to the *Golden Globe*. BB paid attention to how the shuttle craft worked on the way back just in case he had to make a quick getaway and use one.

BB could not shake his feeling of dread. That bothered him even more because his common sense was in full alert mode now. He had been clever in tackling issues with Sparky in the past, even if it was awkward, and he had always succeeded. Never had he felt like maybe this was one of those things that was too much to handle. These characters went on scavenger hunts throughout the cosmos and had brought back a "seed" from something that was nasty as hell. The basic function of a seed is to grow something similar to its origin elsewhere. How could he stop that from happening? Chances were he could not. It was that simple.

"Welcome back, BB," the client said. "It has been acting up."

"How so?" BB asked. His gut tightened a bit more.

"Color from inside the seed has pulsated and changed hue rapidly and it continues to grow larger."

"That is not good. What are the characteristics of the force field and physical containment?" BB said.

"We tried increasing the strength of the magnetic force field and that angered it. In fact, it may have stimulated it, so we backed off. The bulkheads are thick, so it should contain a blast if there is one."

"Are you hearing this, CC?"

"Yes, I am. I don't like the sound of it. What are you going to do or try?" CC said.

"I've got a hypnotic program on Sparky. I've used it on a few bots and people from time to time. It has a 1-10 range. I've never used it above a 3. If I can hook into the force field generator, I might distract the seed from germinating. It's a desperation shot, but what the hell?"

The client understood and encouraged BB to try it. The client also became a bit more frantic.

"I agree, why not... it's probably going to blow anyway," CC said.

"Do I detect sarcasm, CC?" BB said.

Laughter came out of BB's comm unit.

"Hey! Just don't piss it off. If we have to run for it in the *Peregrine*, we'll be slow and an easy target, don't forget."

The client brought BB into the control cabin for the security setup. It showed him the magnetic force field generator. BB set up Sparky and hooked it into the generator. "OK. Here we go. I'm going to hit the go button here and what should happen is brain wave modulators should flood the room. I'm going to level 10. It should put the seed in la-la land. If it germinates, we should all leave the area. Here we go..." BB pushed his trusted button on Sparky. Sounds came out of the compartment. BB and the client looked through the viewport. *KABOOM*!

CHAPTER FIFTEEN

"Listen up everyone." Sophia proceeded to give her crew an update on everything that happened and what to expect next. She wanted them to know Manchester was to blame for everything and that Booster Bob had nothing to do with it.

"Boss." Gwynn, her third in command who ran all the crews that made the Merry-Go-Round perform, stepped forward. "We all wanted to compliment you on outsmarting Manchester's assassination attempt. You have our appreciation for shooting the shit out of him and his crew and for fighting to keep the Merry-Go-Round going round and round. We love our commander and our jobs."

"Well, that is a little thick, but thank you all for working so hard getting the place back together again so quickly so that they did not distract our clients for long. In fact, I suspect most of them thought it was part of the show. Some show, eh? I'm going to take the *Scorpion* and catch up to our recovery ship, the *Saint Bernard*, on its way out to retrieve Zedjack. I don't expect another attack, so the *Blade* plus the heavy weapons on the Merry-Go-Round should keep you all safe until I get back. I'm going to retrieve Booster Bob. He owes me."

Snickering arose from the staff. They knew Sophia wanted what she paid him for... his services.

"Keep a sharp lookout. Oh! One more thing. For security reasons, I've hired Quiver to help with security while I am away. He's a weapons runner, if you don't know him, and his ship is his brand, lots of high-tech firepower. In exchange, I will pay his and his crew's tab."

Everyone laughed as if these threats and bloody exchanges were a sideshow or something. Sophia turned around in a whirl toward the exit bays. A while later, the *Scorpion* unlocked from the Merry-Go-Round and headed out toward the asteroid field.

Sophia arrived on the scene of the damaged *Avenger*. Zedjack's ship looked worse than it was, which was a break for Sophia. The *Saint Bernard* connected to the *Avenger*. All the welding made it look like an exotic Christmas tree with stuttering flashes of light going off on all sides. They repaired the primary systems using modular switched parts despite the heavy damage. Out of a crew of twenty, two were dead and five injured. They transferred the dead and injured to the *Saint Bernard*. Engines were replaced and all other systems tied back together. Zedjack turned the *Avenger* around and headed back home to the Merry-Go-Round accompanied by the *Saint Bernard*. Sophia inspected the debris fields of the Stoners' ships. "Damn. It has to be BB, I'll bet." She knew Manchester was following the *Peregrine*, so she set her ship on the vector the tracer provided. Into the Black Wall the *Scorpion* flew. It all motivated Sophia. Her emotions were in full bloom. She was angry.

The *Scorpion* had a crew of ten, including herself. Half were freebots like herself, the other half were mostly humans with various upgrades. Manchester's trail headed for the void. Sophia knew about the Black Wall, the curtain. It was a visual mystery that absorbed light, but was not a black hole. You could fly into it for sure, but no one knew how big it was or what was on the other side. Many outlaws had disappeared into it, never to be seen again. Most likely, they used it as a getaway. It worked because most would not dare cross it because no one knew how vast it was or what waited for them on the other side. The few who returned told stories of a hostile environment where things wanted to eat you. She smiled at that... the unknown had always frightened humans. Sophia found it curious and exciting. If Manchester dared to cross it, then she would too.

Manchester chuckled to himself. He had been way ahead of everybody else in spotting the *Peregrine* as a treasure trove. He didn't know what the cargo was, but it had stirred up enough gossip to warrant placing a tracer on the hull when it connected to the Merry-Go-Round. So even though his takeover of the Merry-Go-Round failed, he could still go after the *Peregrine*'s cargo while he was figuring out how to go after Sophia again. Booster Bob's getaway on the *Peregrine* was an unfortunate coincidence, but it didn't make any difference now. Manchester knew Sophia would come looking for him to settle the score. They were true enemies. They never rested. Maybe he'd surprise her for a change.

The vector showed the *Peregrine* had made a jump into the void, the Black Wall, the darkness; it had many names. All he could do was follow the last direction the tracer showed, hoping it maintained that direction all the way across. Manchester had nothing to lose. If he got lost, he'd just retrace his steps and write it off as a lost opportunity. He could swing by the asteroid field and pick up what was left of the Stoners so he could return and hit the Merry-Go-Round again when she least expected it. He knew it would take some time for Sophia to show up and help Zedjack out, so he knew he had time on his side. "Line us up with the direction of the tracer and let's make a jump or two and see where we end up."

His crew prepared for the jump and started it. The first time, they ended up still in the void. The second and third time, it was completely black, but on the fourth, they saw stars, universes, and gasses.

"Great job, crew. Welcome to the other side," Manchester said.

You could see and hear his crew members exhale. They had all done some crazy dangerous things with Manchester, but crossing the

Black Wall was like jumping off a cliff, not knowing what was down below. A hairy stunt, but they made it alive.

"Scan for the tracer and see if we can pick up the *Peregrine*'s trail," he said. Within fifteen minutes, they had it not that far off. As Manchester fine-tuned his trajectory ready to sneak up on the cargo freighter, a bright flash of an explosion lit up his scanners and his viewports. "What the hell was that?"

"Sir, it looks like it is very near the *Peregrine*, but not from it. There must be something else near the *Peregrine*," Pyrex, Manchester's second in command, said.

"Any damage to the *Peregrine?*" Manchester asked.

"Can't tell for sure, sir. It looks intact on the scanners. The other craft looks like a giant sphere that the explosion has affected. How bad? Still too far away to tell for sure."

"Alright, let's go in slowly and not draw any attention. I am betting on them being focused on the explosion and the damage, so they won't notice us sneak up in the background. Go easy."

CHAPTER SIXTEEN

STUNNED, CC had a nosebleed from smacking her face against the viewport as she was thrown across the command deck. She picked herself up off the deck. Nothing bleeding or broken, that was good.

"That damn seed must have exploded." She watched as Beatrice ran diagnostics on herself to see if she had sustained any damage as she, too, got back up onto her feet. All green lights. They both ran to the viewport and looked out.

"Let's take care of ourselves first. Damage report!" she barked over the comm system. "Beatrice, see if anything important is broken or compromised. I'll try to contact BB." CC worried about her own ship and crew, but she dreaded finding out what happened to BB on the *Golden Globe*. Debris was flowing out of a gaping hole in the sphere's top. Or was that smoke, or something else?

"BB, do you copy?" Beatrice said repeatedly.

No response. Two minutes passed, nothing, then five minutes.

Coughing boomed into the control deck.

"Is that you, BB?" she said, not believing her ears. "Are you OK? What happened? Where are you?"

"Cough. Cough. Please, one question at a time," BB croaked.

"I can't believe you are alive after that blast. How did you survive that?"

"I am not sure, to be honest. When I fired up Sparky, everything turned bad quickly. Instead of the hypnotic algorithm soothing the seed, it did just the opposite. I swear it looked like the seed had been waiting for it. It germinated before our eyes... I'd call it an explosion or rapid expansion, but it popped. All the force went out instead of in, so we are all banged up, but not injured. Did you miss me?" BB said, trying to be funny.

"Ha! Sure I miss you. I expected to see you floating by like a piece of space junk, but there you are alive and all smartass like. Guess your magic box turned out to be a detonator."

"That's an accurate description. I'm not sure why. Maybe it was just waiting for some form of energy to trigger it. I don't know, but it sure blew."

"What is that sound? Almost like howling..." CC said.

"It's getting louder," BB said. "The sound is coming from our sprout. It's roaring. There's a really foul smell too, like something rotting. I need to move my butt out of here like now. Your client suffered a cracked screen. The blast, or I should say the germination did that. He needs a new face. They are isolating this area to keep it from destroying the rest of the ship. Talk to you soon," BB said, and clicked off.

CC stared at the gaping hole in the *Golden Globe*. She saw lights flashing from the compartment. A mist or cloud was pouring out of it. It wasn't dissipating. It was coagulating.

CC directed Beatrice, "Run a scan of that blob and tell me its makeup."

"Organic molecules, multiple strands of amino acids.....it looks like a protein," Beatrice said.

"So we're dealing with some kind of nasty living thing that is growing out of control. Wish we had some weed killer."

"Was that intended as a joke?" Beatrice asked.

CC laughed. "Yes, Beatrice. That was sarcasm as a joke."

"Oh. That..." Beatrice said as she shifted her attention back to the viewport.

"CC... are you there?" BB said over the comm system.

"I'm here. What's your status over there?"

"We're on the other side of the ship. The Aggregators are upset. Their hobby has turned into a life-threatening creature. They are trying to get all of it outside their ship. It's my fault, I guess. Trying to help them control this thing with Sparky was just what it needed to germinate and boy, did it ever pop. There's no way I could have known it would backfire like this."

"Not your fault, BB. They asked for your help and you tried. Get this, there is an ejection of organic material coming out of the blown compartment hole into space. We analyzed it and it reads like a protein, lots of amino acids. Has it sprouted into an animal?"

"I just told your client that and he is freaking out, screaming all kinds of orders to his crew, none of which I understand. If I'm reading them right, it seems this seed has germinated and is getting ready to feed itself off protein contained inside the seed itself. They are afraid that if it grows and matures, it will turn into another monster like the one they ran into when they picked up the seed."

"That's not good. I could start blasting at it from here, but I will not do that with you onboard, plus your host might not appreciate it either."

"That's thoughtful of you," BB said, chuckling. "I need to get back to the *Peregrine*. We may need to make a run for it. Any ideas on how I can do that?"

"I'll send Beatrice over in a shuttle to pick you up now."

"Fine. I'll make my apologies for blowing up their ship and bug out. Did the blast break anything on the *Peregrine*?"

"Not really. A bunch of stuff fell off shelves. A few people suffered minor injuries because of the shockwave, but we're OK. Anything we can do for them?"

"I'll ask, but they are busy defending themselves right now. See you soon."

CC caught her breath as she watched BB scramble out of the shuttlecraft. He looked like a burnt potato chip. "Whoa... you look a little singed around the edges."

"Yeah, well, I'm lucky to be here. I can't believe how I've made everything worse. I thought for sure my genius could bring calm to a throbbing seed. Sparky gave it just what it was looking for and triggered an explosive germination."

"Should we try to help them?"

"We should delay for a short while until they decide what they want to do. I feel obligated, but not to the point of putting us all in more danger than we are already in. Let me see if I can get them to talk to us."

CC said. "Beatrice, see if you can raise them on channel 1 or 2."

Beatrice reached out "This is the *Peregrine* calling the *Golden Globe*. Is anybody over there able to talk to us?"

Silence. Beatrice repeated... then they could hear a crackle.

"Yes, *Peregrine*, we hear you." The client's face had a piece of what looked like tape across his screen to keep it from falling out. "It is still frantic here, but we have tried to jettison this pest physically out of the room it blew out. It seems intent on doing that anyway, so we're trying to help it by channeling a bunch of nasty stuff into the compartment,"

CC said, "So if you're successful in getting it out of your ship, then what are you going to do?"

"Run in the opposite direction as fast as we can. This thing will become way more vile as it gets bigger. We've seen its parents up close, and they are terrifying."

BB said, "I am so sorry my attempt to control the seed with Sparky backfired. Is there anything we can do to help you?"

"You were trying to help. It was not your fault. We have been collecting for a very long time. This is the first time that an artifact has almost killed us. Time to review our project goals, assuming we survive this."

There was that phrase again. *It was not your fault. Maybe I should get out of this business*, BB wondered.

"*POOF!*"

CC jumped. "What was that? Wait, a second. It looks like the weed is out of your compartment. That's a good thing, right?"

"Indeed, it is... we wanted it out of there and I think it wanted out too, so together we've succeeded. We're going to back off slowly at first and then speed out of here."

"We've got company, I'm afraid," BB said.

"What?" the client said.

"It's another one of those Anglerfish that you saved us from when we first arrived. It looks like it's focusing on the evil sprout. This should be interesting."

Comm channels fell silent as all eyes watched the Anglerfish dance around the sprout, dangling its flashing oscillating lure in front of it. At first, the sprout was confused. The Anglerfish grew more aggressive and came closer, which was a dumb move. Tentacle extensions shot out so fast that you could hear gasps around the room. Sprout grabbed the lure and pulled the entire Anglerfish inside of itself in one quick movement. Organic feeding on organic. It was all over in seconds.

"OK, then. I'd say it's time to get away from this thing because we all have organic people on both ships that this weed is going to sniff out once it gets hungry again," CC said.

CHAPTER SEVENTEEN

MANCHESTER WATCHED FROM A DISTANCE. Something had gone wrong on the ship that looked like a golden ball. An internal explosion had ruptured a hole in it and something was flowing out of it. The *Peregrine* did not show any signs of damage externally. He didn't want to turn on any of his scanners, since that would give away their position. So for now, watching from a distance would have to do. A shuttlecraft left the *Peregrine* and traveled over to the globe. Within minutes, it returned to the *Peregrine*.

Manchester surmised *Peregrine*'s cargo was now in the hands of its client in the damaged ship. What was it? Could it have caused the explosion? Why? He was growing impatient, waiting. It was against his nature to remain in doubt with his prey so close, but he told himself he had to hold off a little while longer.

"What the hell is that thing?" CC whispered as she stared from the viewport. "Obviously, it has to eat. I think that's apparent. It seems to prefer organic matter rather than rocket ships or we'd all be gone by now. What happens when organic matter is not available?" CC tilted her head to the side, looking at BB.

The mic was open on the comm channel, and the client spoke up, "We think it propagates organic material almost like a garden. It could live forever, like the Anglerfish, with an organic source of sustenance."

"It grows organic material and harvests it when it needs energy. This sprout now has all it needs to grow and grow without starving out?" CC surmised.

"Precisely. It will now expand to an enormous size like its mother and generate radiation and lightning as defenses. It doesn't bother robots, but it is deadly to organics. We had to stay a great distance away from it for that reason," the client said. "The only positive thing is that, to our knowledge, it does not travel. It stays put, but it will start launching seed pods to propagate itself."

"This gigantic piece of crabgrass tossed a seed your way, you went for it. Why?"

"Fascination and curiosity... perhaps a flaw in our species. We're leaving now. Thank you for delivering the seed to us. When we discovered the seed pod attached to our ship, it was dormant and seemed harmless. It was fortunate it did not germinate while you were transporting it."

"I agree with that," CC said. "The clientele on the Merry-Go-Round would have been upset if they ended up being dinner for the sprout."

"Goodbye my friends," the client said. The Golden Globe pulled back slowly from the sprout, who was digesting its dinner of Anglerfish. The further the Golden Globe moved, the more it sped up. It faded into the black.

"I think we should do the same," BB said.

"Beatrice, get us out of here," Before Beatrice could follow CC's order, they heard a dull thump. The *Peregrine* shuddered. "What the hell is going on here? Somebody is firing on us. Zigzag maneuver! Defense shields up. Everyone to your guns!"

CC wondered why they didn't hit them directly with their first shot since they had no shields up at all. Strange, maybe it was just a holdup attempt.

Manchester fired another shot near the *Peregrine*. Blowing the *Peregrine* to pieces wasn't what he wanted to do, just shake it up some so he could come aboard and see if there was any valuable treasure left inside. He couldn't care less what the stringy plant looking mass was or why it blew itself out of the side of the golden ball. There was still a possibility that the rumored treasure cargo might still be on the *Peregrine*. The *Revenge* moved closer to the *Peregrine*. As he reached about half the distance to the *Peregrine*, it came to life and fired a surprising barrage at him. Startled, Manchester was not fast enough to increase his shield's strength before the incoming fire tore into his shield and penetrated it. Damage was done, but nothing significant.

"What have we here? This is not a normal freighter. Scans show they have some respectable defensive hardware onboard that thing. Makes me think they might also have some cargo they want to protect as well. Let's see if we can convince them they need to give it to us."

"*Peregrine*? Oh, *Peregrine*? Are you there?" No answer. "Innocent, defenseless big freighter with something valuable onboard. Oh! Come on! Who are you kidding? There is something on board I want. You wouldn't have that kind of firepower if you were an average freighter. You and I both know that," Manchester yelled.

"Who the hell is that?" BB said off the mic to CC.

"That, if I'm not mistaken, is Mr. Manchester doing what he does best, robbing and destroying. He's our neighborhood bully," CC said.

"Give him the bowling ball," BB said.

"What? The hell I will. Not my bowling ball?" CC said.

"Now it's your bowling ball, is it? Listen! We seem to be in a predicament here if you haven't noticed. Make the crystal ball seem like our big secret valuable cargo. Get it?"

"I hear what you're saying. I just don't want to do it. Aw shit, OK, fine! Damn it!"

Oh, she was angry, extremely angry, close to rage. He knew he didn't have time to worry about her emotional attachment to the damned thing with Manchester focused on them.

"This is Booster Bob speaking. Who is there?"

"I am Mr. Manchester to you. Wait a second, are you Booster Bob, the one who destroyed Sophia back on the Merry-Go-Round?"

Interesting, BB thought. *How would he know anything about that if he was not involved?* "For starters, I figured out how I was used to make it look like I killed Sophia. Are you responsible?"

"I could be. Then again, it might be just scuttlebutt. So what?" Manchester demanded.

"So how do you even know about Sophia's demise unless you just came from the Merry-Go-Round? Since you've failed to take over the MGR several times, you have the motive to set me up as the one who murdered Sophia. Is that what happened? That way, no one would suspect you."

Manchester said nothing.

Realizing his questions were not going to be answered, BB returned to the business at hand. "We realize there is no good way out of this predicament we find ourselves in and are more than willing to hand over the prize if you promise not to kill us all."

"Why give up so easily... without a fight?" Manchester said.

"Fine! We can do it your way. Down to the last person. Take no prisoners. No rules, just one aim: eliminate the other," BB bluffed.

Manchester thought a while, in no rush. He walked up closer to the console. "That won't be necessary. Show me the prize I've earned for not incinerating you."

"I'm not the captain, but I have her word that this is what she will offer. She is not happy about it." BB reached outside the video's view and pulled the bowling ball bag into view. BB said nothing.

"Are you making fun of me?"

"No. I am not making fun of you. This is the valuable cargo we are carrying." As BB pulled the bowling ball out of its carrying case and sat it on top of the control panel, it sparked to life with light and sound, twirling like a merry-go-round. BB felt that was so appropriate for the situation. When it stopped spinning, it became a mirror of the control room, BB, CC and even Manchester.

"What's with the grumpy one on the big screen?" Bruster Bill asked from inside the bowling ball.

"He wants to take you with him," was all that BB said.

BB's duplicate didn't flinch. He didn't care. He had no loyalties to anyone, just a job to do in his world, and that was all he cared about. Manchester's body language changed. He came closer to the screen to get a better look at the thing.

"So what is it?" Manchester said.

"It is a portal into a parallel universe. They seem far more advanced than we are in technologies, warfare, and civilizations," BB said, going full bluff.

Manchester drew even closer to the screen. BB brought the bowling ball nearer to the camera. BB amazed Manchester with his doppelgänger in the sphere. His ego wanted to know what he was doing in that parallel world.

"So what's it like over there on your side?" Manchester said.

"About the same and yet different," Manchester's duplicate said.

BB could tell Manchester knew what his voice sounded like, and it seemed to astound him at how identical it was coming from himself in another universe. Now he knew Manchester's mind was being changed. BB watched in fascination as Manchester's alter ego on the other side influenced him. The same thing had happened with CC's admiration for how much better she looked in the mirror. He was impressed with the duplicate's ability to read Manchester's personality. It was instant and accurate, but BB felt it was the mock sincerity that won the exchange. Manchester was hooked.

"OK. I'll take it. How do you want to deliver it to me?" Manchester said.

"Your shuttle or ours, it doesn't make any difference to us," BB said.

KABOOM!

"Your shuttle or ours, it doesn't make any difference to us," BB said.

KABOOM!

CHAPTER EIGHTEEN

Sophia's ship popped out of the Black Wall intact. She turned on all the sophisticated sensors she had to pick up on Manchester's trail. It was not long before she picked up his direction. She plotted a jump as far out as her sensors could see and kept doing that until she picked up multiple ships and something in front of her. None of them had sensors looking her way, so she moved in slowly to a distance where she could see what was going on.

"Zoom in on the group first with visual magnification," Sophia ordered. It was a strange situation. There was a large organic object near the two ships and a golden ball ship limping away, leaving debris behind. Son-of-a-bitch! She ran profile checks on the remaining two ships on her ship's ID library. Sure enough, that was Manchester's *Revenge* and the *Peregrine*. He looked like he was trying to shake them down for their treasure cargo. "Attention, gunners, give Mr. Manchester a knock on the door." She saw in a reflection on a surface that her face had turned metallic blue; robot rage, she called it. She felt both startled and pleased. She had not felt this level of rage in a very long time and it was difficult for a robot to show it.

While Manchester had his shields up as a precaution, they were not at full power. A volley of fire hit the back end of his fighter with full force. It shook the *Revenge* and filled it with sound. *KABOOM!* Manchester disappeared from the communicator scene as his ship rocked. BB and CC looked on, both their mouths agape.

"What just happened?" BB said.

Manchester popped back up into the view on the screen. "Who the hell is that shooting at me?" he screamed.

"It's not us!" BB yelled back. "I don't know where that came from."

Manchester's head swung to one side as if he were looking at something, "She has found me. I cannot believe it. Fucking machines!"

The screen went black. The *Peregrine* saw Manchester's ship flying overhead and behind them, using *Peregrine* as a shield from the incoming fire.

"What should we do?" BB said to CC.

"I say do nothing. We don't want to become a casualty in the middle of this crossfire, and not moving might improve our chances of survival," CC answered.

"That makes sense." BB flinched from a near miss. "How come all this incoming fire is going around us instead of through us?"

"Ship profile lock-on. It means whoever is going after Manchester has locked onto the *Revenge*'s profile, so when a missile arrives here and sees the *Peregrine*, it knows it is not the target. It goes around us and keeps looking for the profile until it finds it," CC said.

"Kind of like a smart bullet. I'm impressed," BB said. "Somebody is serious about blowing Manchester away. Can't say I'm upset about that after what I think he did to me and now with him trying to shake us down for our.... your bowling ball."

CC squealed with delight. "Yes! I get to keep it, don't I? It's very important to me."

"I know... we need to have a talk about that, but later," BB said.

Another missile swung wide, barely missing the *Peregrine* in its pursuit of Manchester. BB wondered who the pursuer could be. If it was Zedjack, head of the MGR's security team, why target

Manchester instead of BB? It made no sense. His gaze locked onto the huge green thing not far off. What a mess. He had tried to work his special magic with Sparky, and instead, he had unleashed a giant piece of undulating crabgrass. He believed he'd lost his touch, his edge, but he also knew failure was part of the process of creating anything new.

———

"Hey! Booster Bob! Are you in there?"

The *Scorpion*, which had been pounding Manchester as he hobbled away, came next to *Peregrine*… real close. It was still firing away into the distance, but it was not in hot pursuit now.

BB stood up and turned toward the view windows that showed the sleek black medium cruiser almost at a full stop. They had caught him was his first thought, but another part of him was confused and even wondered for a minute if he recognized the voice. That was silly.

"Booster Bob! You owe me one," the voice said on all channels.

CC froze, clutching her bowling ball even tighter. She looked at BB, searching for answers. He was just as confused as she was.

BB could not think of anything clever to say. Was he caught or not? "Yes. This is Booster Bob. Sophia? That can't be you."

The big screen popped on, and all he saw was someone with a helmet-mounted display covering their face. "Oh! It's me alright. I want my money's worth. You skipped town on me." She flipped off the display, and there she was, the one and only, sort of, Sophia.

BB could hear that chuckle that was only hers. The one she had somehow mastered, because everybody knew robots couldn't snicker or chuckle. "Sophia! It is you. You can't be real. I watched you disintegrate before my very eyes." Tears ran down BB's cheeks.

"That's right, and what was the last thing I said to you?"

"You said it wasn't my fault."

"Damn right… and it was not your fault. It was that fucking bastard Manchester who set you up as the patsy."

"I figured out most of it while I was escaping with Commander Cody here," BB said.

"Yes. And I figured out the same thing while I was rejuvenating myself back on the Merry-Go-Round. Nano-bots in my hydraulic fluid that released acid on cue."

"Exactly," BB said. "So you came all the way out here to tell me this?"

"Well, not exactly, but everything pointed in the same direction. Manchester and I had a brief exchange on the Merry-Go-Round when he thought I was dead, so he tried to take over the place. I ran him off, but he had heard the rumors about Commander Cody's cargo being special. He got a tracer slapped onto the hull so he could find the *Peregrine* later."

There was a loud thump as CC dropped her bowling ball. "He did what?" CC said, turning bright red.

"What was that noise?" Sophia asked.

"Oh, nothing. Just me dropping something heavy."

"That's what he does: murder, robbery and mayhem... a true predator. Don't take it personally, CC. He's good at what he does," Sophia said. "The real fluke was BB jumping onto the *Peregrine* to make his getaway. My security chief, Zedjack, took off after BB and ran into Manchester at the asteroid field where someone had wasted most of the Stoners hiding there."

Now it was BB's turn to turn red. "Yeah, that was my doing," BB said.

"You? What the hell?"

"He is extraordinary on the gatling gun. I've never seen anything like it. Neither had the Stoners. He's a natural," CC added.

"BB! You are racking up points with me here. So Manchester figures out that I'm telling on him to Zedjack while they're facing each other, so he mauls *Avenger* badly and keeps on after the *Peregrine*. I got Zedjack's cruiser patched up enough so he can limp back to the Merry-Go-Round. And then I took off looking for both of you, Manchester and BB."

"First, I am so happy to see you again alive, plus with a few upgrades," BB said.

Sophia laughed. "Call it progress. They are based on your preferences, you know."

Again, BB generated color and heat because of embarrassment. "OK. Second, I apologize for creating this mess..." He gestured toward the monster plant growing bigger by the second off in the distance.

"It wasn't his fault again," CC said. "My client collected this seed from somewhere in the cosmos. Aggregators, a race of gatherers, and they contacted me to deliver it along with a bunch of other stuff. They moved it secretly using several back channels and me. Don't ask me why. I don't ask questions. They had trouble with the seed after we unloaded it into their golden sphere. It came alive and became agitated. BB thought his Sparky might soothe it, and instead, it activated the damn thing and it germinated, blowing out a compartment on their ship."

"BB, you've been very busy as usual," Sophia said. "You tried to help, and it didn't work. So what?"

"It just seems that lately everything I touch melts down or blows up. I will say the marksmanship thing was a pleasant surprise to me, an unknown skill set I enjoyed discovering. Had to come from all the game-playing I did when I was a kid."

A spray of laser cannons hit both the *Peregrine* and *Scorpion*. Shields were up so no damage, but Manchester was coming back at them.

"Well, Manchester doesn't like surprises, and he's had several in a brief period. Looks like we're in for a fight. BB! Get on that gatling gun and show me what you can do. CC, we would appreciate any help. He's got me outgunned, but maybe with the both of us, we can frustrate him."

"He already has sniffed the *Peregrine* out, so he knows we have more punch than you would expect from a freighter. Let's see what we all can do. Battle stations everyone," CC said.

"Sophia, I owe you so much in so many ways. If we get through this, I will give you a session you'll never forget," BB said.

Sophia raised her eyebrows, wrinkled her nose and said with a smile, "Now that's something worth fighting for. I look forward to it."

Because Sophia's *Scorpion* was smaller and could move faster, she shot off to the left of the *Peregrine*. This forced Manchester to deal with two targets, not just one. BB jumped back into the seat of the gatling gun and fired off a volley.

Sophia, BB and CC concentrated all the firepower they had on Manchester's *Revenge*. He started jumping around to avoid incoming fire. That was when BB remembered an old skill he had developed while playing video games. Anticipation. Could he accurately guess where Manchester would jump to before he made a jump? Only one way to find out. BB focused on Manchester's pattern. Sure enough, there was a pattern, so BB started firing into those locations just before Manchester arrived. Manchester got smacked every time he jumped. It happened so fast, he could not get off a shot. Not once, but every time, it blasted his damaged shields. Manchester was losing his defense system, and he was not doing any damage to the *Peregrine* or *Scorpion* because he didn't have enough time to get off a shot.

BB, CC and Sophia watched as Manchester's *Revenge* gave up and made its getaway, trailing debris. "I'd say it is time for a little celebration," CC said. "Sophia, bring your crew over and we'll toast to our new superstar, Booster Bob. I've never seen shooting like that before in the entire galaxy. Break out some beverages, please."

Sophia accepted the invitation and arrived with her crew. After she entered the lounge, she stopped and stared at BB. "My friend, that was some fancy shooting you just did."

"Thank you," BB said. "It's like a cognitive and perceptive sense that I can't direct, but I have it just the same."

"I'm glad you are on our side. I may have to collect that debt you owe me after the party. You are turning me on without even trying." She walked over to him and embraced him.

BB turned crimson. Sophia kissed BB, and CC laughed. They all agreed that Manchester would not be back to visit them. His *Revenge* had suffered damage, as his shields flickered on and off. He needed to get away, which he did. While they knew he would not be back, they also knew he would make repairs and soon head back to the Merry-Go-Round for one last try to take it.

CHAPTER NINETEEN

As the party began, BB stood by a large viewing port and stared at the monster he had helped bring to life. It undulated in slow motion like kelp in an ocean he saw a very long time ago when he was younger. There was a big difference. The scale of this thing was maybe ten times what he remembered. Plus it had long, quick arms that could grab, slash and tear. He felt responsible. He was worried it might never have sprouted had he not triggered it. Like a seed in the sand in the desert waiting for that one drop of water that brings it to life, BB was that water drop, and he regretted it.

CC walked up behind him. "Remember, my client asked for help. You gave it. The damn thing popped anyway. So now we either do something with it or maybe we don't... we could just leave it behind."

"I know, but I hate playing the role of catalyst these days. Same thing happened when I fried Sophia, even though that was not my fault; regardless, I triggered it. Guess maybe that's my new brand. BB the Trigger."

"Please. Don't be so maudlin." Sophia joined them. "You have not had enough to drink yet. So, CC, what's the story with your client? Are they like space beachcombers?"

"Excellent description. Yes, they call themselves the 'Aggregators.'

They roam the cosmos picking up flotsam and jetsam, whatever they find, something that interests them. This one, they should have left alone. Even they knew it when they retrieved the seed. Their curiosity got the better of them."

BB recalled picking up shells at the beach as a child, finding hermit crabs living inside them. He understood the Aggregator's quest, but he also recognized danger when he saw it.

"I do not know what you're talking about," Sophia said. "I had no childhood and the false memories they gave me were terrible and cliche. When I figured out I was a robot, I was relieved and disappointed that I could not have childhood memories. I've been thinking about generating some childhood memories."

BB laughed. "It's OK. We're in mixed company here. We are all of various physical systems, or should I say, physical mechanics?" he said.

"By mixed, you mean robot, cyborg and human?" Sophia said.

"Exactly," BB said.

"Wait, a second. How do you know which of us is one-hundred-percent human versus cyborg?" CC said.

"Determining whether a person is a cyborg is pretty simple," Sophia said. "A quick scan shows you are a cyborg, CC, because of the metal content, while BB is not... not very magical, but accurate."

"When BB was setting me up for my session, I surprised him. When he entered my system to double-check that all was OK and ready to go, I entered his," Sophia said.

BB lit up like a warning beacon, bright red and throbbing. "Alright! Please. No more details," he said.

They all laughed as BB radiated red heat from embarrassment.

"Shocking. BB, how do you do that? Turn that red? I've been trying to replicate it for a very long time. I usually end up damaging myself rather than turning red. My aim was to give BB a sample or reciprocal stimulation, so to speak," Sophia said.

CC's eyebrows rose like caterpillars, smiling and making a *tsk! tsk!* sound. "Maybe you've met your match here, BB. I personally can vouch for him. He is a master, so I can imagine how surprised he was when you showed up unannounced, from the dead," CC said.

Sophia started laughing. "Well, since it seems to be 'tell it all' time, let me just say that while I know full well about Booster Bob's reputation, I've developed a few tricks of my own. Remember, I started out as an 'Oh Honey Baby 1237D model."

Everyone burst into laughter. Having sex in space was almost mandatory because of the long hauls with nothing else to do. Drugs and suspended animation were available, of course, but dangerous or boring. The films, documentaries, series, historical, comedy... etc., were also available, but there was a limit to how much of it you could tolerate. That was how Booster Bob had invented himself. He recognized the need for a neutral person who could walk in, jack into your nervous systems, and blow your sexual mind in half an hour. Where BB surpassed all the others was the fact that he did the homework. He studied how to turn on humans, cyborgs, robots, and other species and to what level. Then he studied combinations and wrote the algorithms for his "Sparky." Over time, he got even better based on feedback. BB was a god among the horny.

"So since I cannot get drunk, I may have to collect on what you owe me, BB," Sophia said.

"I pride myself on satisfaction guaranteed, regardless of interruptions," BB said. "And because of the unfortunate delay, I'm adding a free bonus to your treatment, which will curl your circuit boards."

"Is that an idle threat or a promise?"

"A promise... shall we?"

CC bobbed a curtsy to them both and said, "Normally, I'd tell you two to take it outside, but that's impossible. We'll turn up the music to cover the noise."

BB and Sophia laughed and walked toward a hallway that led to BB's compartment. "I still cannot believe you are alive and well," BB said, thinking out loud.

"You can never have too many backups of yourself. It has saved me more than once. This time, it was very close. When I realized I was disintegrating, I still had time to trigger my double. It's programmed to be automatic, but I never trust it enough to leave it that way. Automatics can fail."

"Makes sense. I feel the same way about Sparky. The script wouldn't be the same if I allowed it to run by itself. I monitor and make adjustments on the fly so I can maximize the experience. It works, or so my customers tell me."

They arrived at BB's compartment. "It's not as fancy as your magnificent palace apartment on the Merry-Go-Round, but it is comfortable. Please lie on the couch and relax. Let me fire up my machine.... pun intended," BB said.

BB loved that Sophia laughed at herself; few robots could master that detachment. It didn't seem to bother her at all. She laid herself out on the couch and got comfortable. BB jacked into the back of her head and then started up all his protocols and checkout connections.

"Oh! There you are again... I wasn't expecting you to enter my system like you did last time," BB said when a little quiver came in his voice.

"This time, I think we should attempt to synchronize. We won't let anyone interrupt us prematurely this time, unlike last time. Hum! I can feel you connecting all over the place. My! You are thorough."

"I try," BB said. He was sure of himself, his programming, and his equipment. What he was nervous about was that this was the first time where a client wanted to stimulate him at the same time. "You have me excited already and I have not even turned your side on yet."

"I say we alternate, tag team it, do solo and in unison and see what happens?" Sophia said. "Are you game?"

"Yes. I am. This will be fresh territory for both of us. I'm open minded and relish diving into the unknown. I'll record the entire session. What could go wrong? I think we both experienced the worst trip last time around with you melting down and me running for my life, so I'm very optimistic this time around. Let's do it?"

BB threw the switch and watched as Sophia sucked in her synthetic lungs like she had touched something freezing. She should be experiencing a flood of warmth, then the light followed, washing over her, and she relaxed. This was going to be wonderful.

———

In an attempt to keep themselves occupied, CC and Beatrice ran maintenance procedures on the *Peregrine*. A high-pitched shriek startled them both. It came from down the passageway, from BB's compartment. They looked at each other for a long moment. Recognition registered on both of their faces, accompanied by smiles.

"I remember that part," Beatrice said.

"So do I," CC said. They resumed their tasks.

Booster Bob arrived first, ricocheting from side to side, trying to walk straight down the hallway. Clothes shredded, but that didn't seem to bother him in the least. His face looked like his "joy button" was stuck in the "on" position. His first attempts to talk were challenging. "I've been... no, she did things... wait, never..." He looked around and smiled. "I think we can make millions off the video recording. I'm sure of it."

Sophia emerged second, stumbling and holding herself up by grabbing on to anything she could lean against. Her body was still all in one piece. The flight suit was not, and she looked almost drunk, which wasn't possible. She stopped, stood up more straight and said, "BB is a genius and a beast. That was out of any realm of experience that I've enjoyed and believe me, I've been around." She sat down in one of the command chairs. Beatrice covered her with a robe she'd pulled out of a locker near the door.

"So who won?" CC asked.

"I think it was a tie," BB said.

CHAPTER TWENTY

MANCHESTER JUMPED up and down in his rage. His high-tech, super sophisticated, lightning fast, over armed *Revenge* resembled a sinking ancient U-boat from a big war long ago. There were fluids spewing; gas jets blowing in all directions; small electrical fires; alarms blaring and warning lights flashing all at once. None of it was serious. It was all repairable and would not take long to fix, but Manchester could not believe that Sophia had shown up at the wrong time yet again. "Give me the details of the damage and how long it'll take to fix everything!" he demanded.

He decided to return to the Merry-Go-Round. She was here and not there. He had destroyed the *Avenger* at the asteroid field. What better time to take it all over while she was not there to protect it?

"Sir, we will complete repairs in two hours. We can make jumps even while we are fixing the minor damage. We can leave at your command, sir," said Manchester's second in command.

"Excellent. Let's see how fast we can get back to the asteroid field. I want to pick up some reinforcements on my way back to the Merry-Go-Round. I want to be in complete control of it by the time Sophia returns," he said.

"Sir, how do you know that Sophia was teaming up with the *Peregrine*?"

"Before it got too hot for us, I caught a good profile image of the surprise attacker. That was her alright. The sensor profile matched the *Scorpion* that protects the Merry-Go-Round. It's a medium cruiser. We blew the *Avenger* and Zedjack away at the edge of the asteroid field so there can't be much of a defense system left to protect the Merry-Go-Round. They'll put up a resistance, but we should be able to force the Merry-Go-Round to surrender without much of a fight."

As Zedjack limped back home to the Merry-Go-Round on the *Avenger*, he marveled at what a sweet sight it was to come home to after all. The MGR was more than what it appeared to be. It was a bright-colored jewel spinning in the vastness of space. It was like an old-time truck stop where travelers could have their vehicle repaired, refueled and then drop their loose credits while having some fun. Contact with others in a social space was rare this far out on the edge of the galaxy. He had to hand it to Sophia. She had kept it interesting. There were other competitors out here, but the MGR was one of a kind and Zedjack loved it.

Zedjack's *Avenger* was being repaired in the belly of the Merry-Go-Round in Sophia's advanced engineering lab. He marveled at the sophistication and speed of the automated process. Spare parts were being manufactured in three-dimensional replicators as needed. Zedjack was eager to get his *Avenger* fully operational again. Manchester had bloodied his nose and damn near obliterated him and his crew at the edge of the asteroid field with an old trick that he should have recognized. But it was more than that. With Sophia off searching for both Booster Bob and the *Peregrine*, the Merry-Go-Round was vulnerable. The sooner he could get his *Avenger* up and running, the better defense they had against Manchester, who could show up again and try to take it over again. They were still short of a medium cruiser, the *Scorpion*. Sophia had taken it, but they still had the *Blade*, another medium cruiser. Regardless, they would still be a little light on the perimeter. He needed to find another edge. Something Manchester would not expect. Once they repaired the *Avenger*, they camouflaged it in the MGR's superstructure so no one would know the *Avenger* was there and ready to fight.

There was another system Zedjack remembered Sophia talking about that could give him an early warning when Manchester showed up. He was sure it was still in the prototype stage, but if he could deploy it successfully, he would have the early warning of any visitors or enemies. It was a sphere of super sensitive sensor particles so small, a single one looked like a grain of sand. Because of the extremely small size, it was undetectable. They could position them out from the Merry-Go-Round three times the normal distance of most security perimeters. Exactly what Zedjack needed. He contacted the engineering team and told them to find it, and start working on it. He asked his security team to look into how Manchester bypassed their security last time. They changed all codes, passwords, networks and physical locks. There had to be a key or someone on the inside. That was what he feared most: a mole or a conspirator. Zedjack was determined to flush him or her out.

———

"So this was given to CC by her client or I should say she weaseled it out of him before he had to leave in a hurry." BB held up the bowling ball bag like a trophy.

"Oh! That?" CC responded, as if surprised by it being there. "Um... well, it's a little prize I talked my client out of before the seed germinated."

"So tell me about it, but first, do you have an extra set of clothes? BB turned into a bit of a beast and shredded most of mine," she said.

"You should talk," BB offered in defense as he twirled 360°, showing off the tattered remains of his outfit.

"You two really should take it outside. I'm serious. Guess we'll have to get you some new state-of-the-art crew jumpsuits. Beatrice, can you take care of them? When you get back, Sophia, I'll show you my prize," CC said.

Beatrice stood up and motioned for both BB and Sophia to follow her down one of the passageways leading off the command deck. They followed her.

BB's mind still vibrated from the sensory overload that Sophia had introduced him to during their foray into... what? It was supposed to be a late payback for services paid for, but it went way beyond that for sure. He had concentrated on putting together an advanced program on Sparky. After all, he felt like he owed her something special after all that had happened and the trouble she had gone to in finding him. Sophia had surprised him by again waiting for him when he entered her system for verification of hookup and sync. So what started out as a customer satisfaction event morphed into a sexual orgy that was extraordinary. They had recorded it for history. He smiled.

"So something is making you smile?"

"I am only now capable of verbalizing the impact you had on me back there when we, you know, we were doing our thing. I expected to be the maestro of the concert, but it turned into a battle of the bands. You have a talented band," BB said.

Sophia smiled broadly. "I tried some new ideas and you seemed to like them. For me, the experience was extraordinary. You surprised me at every turn with another sensation, emotion or vision I wasn't expecting or didn't know was possible. The way you blended them was yummy... some individually and others all at once. It took my breath away, and that's saying something since I don't breathe."

BB laughed.

Beatrice led them into a locker room compartment where flight suits, jumpsuits and space suits hung around the entire room off the walls. Both of them picked red flight suits. They got rid of what they left of their old clothes and zipped into the new ones.

Once they returned to the command deck, BB asked, "CC, I know you want to show Sophia your new toy, but the monster out there keeps growing. Should we try to destroy it, tow it, or just leave it?"

"We've been watching it closely. It's self-perpetuating. So far, it has not started ejecting seed pods like the one it hatched from, but I'm guessing that will occur eventually."

"Sophia, what do you think we should do about it?" CC said.

"Unless it presents an imminent threat, I'm not sure I'd do anything. It would be a great attraction back at the Merry-Go-Round, but how would we get it back home? Nope. We could leave a warning for others." Sophia said. "I don't know how many other folks are living out here. Your client is not coming back, that's for sure, so who is in the neighborhood? Not much left besides those angler creatures, and they seem to work well for food. I say leave it be and let's get back to the Merry-Go-Round. Manchester has to be heading there as well by now."

CHAPTER TWENTY-ONE

ZEDJACK WAS busy running the Merry-Go-Round business and preparing for an imminent arrival and attack by Manchester. Maybe he was exaggerating to himself how serious the threat was in reality, but after almost losing his ship, his crew and himself to this bastard... "No. You're not doing enough," he said out loud to himself. "Keep driving hard. It will pay off in the end."

After grinding through four-day cycles, Zedjack had a successful day. Three events occurred.

His team uncovered Manchester's undetected security breach. It wasn't a person; it was a device. They called them "parasites" and they literally lived on the host. They also gave the user an inside ear to everything that was going on in the Merry-Go-Round. Someone had smuggled it onboard and attached it to the core nervous system of the Merry-Go-Round. When detected and confronted, this device could duplicate a nearby connection and function so it would appear as the only one. The only way you could find these was by running wiring diagram comparisons. Bingo!

The parasites gave Manchester passwords for security, so the last time when he came aboard, he breached security easily. Not one gate saw a problem, green lights all the way. Zedjack's security team built countermeasures and tested them across the system. They quarantined Manchester's "parasite" for the time being. He didn't want it disconnected yet. It might be useful if Manchester still thought it was operating undetected.

Number two, they had brought the prototype of the extreme range, non-detectable sensing system back to life and were testing it now. It was still a little buggy, but if they could get it to work properly, they would have an early warning of Manchester's approach without him knowing.

The technicians restored Zedjack's *Avenger* to full combat readiness.

"Yes!" he said. "I want you to park it up close to the Merry-Go-Round so that it looks like it's part of the structure. Throw some paint on it to make it blend in. I don't want the profile to be discernible. Then park the *Blade* out front so everybody can see it." He figured Manchester expected to see just the medium cruiser, and that was exactly what he was going to see.

A message on his communicator interrupted his progress. It was from Sophia. It said, "On my way back. Had run in with Manchester. He's coming back your way and I'm way behind him, but coming fast. Type 'Voila' into the mainframe and hit return. PW: LastresortKaboom4701."

Zedjack felt sweat trickle down his backbone. He recognized the command and the password. Sophia had beaten it into his brain that if this command came to him from her, he was not to hesitate, think about it, or take any pause. He was to sit down in front of a console and do exactly what she requested. Zedjack sat down, typed in "Viola" and then typed in the password when requested. His screen went black, then a cartoonish graphic of "KABOOM!" burst onto the screen for two seconds, and then everything went back to normal.

Sophia had never told him what that command triggered or what to expect afterwards. Zedjack figured she knew what she was doing, so he wouldn't worry about it. He assumed Sophia was preparing for another Manchester takeover.

BB had repaid his debt to Sophia by giving her the best session he could create. The shocker was that she had equaled his performance in doing the same to him. She had called his bet and raised him one. BB was in love.

Was that possible? It was taboo, of course, but he was way past that with his line of business. No laws against it, but some folks did not approve. BB chuckled. He remembered reading history about how some folks thought spending money on the first landing of a man on the moon was a waste. What would they think now?

After thousands of years, humans still had a hard time with pleasure. If it felt good, it was probably bad or sinful or both. There were religions built on that premise. Eventually, religions became superfluous, except for the cults. But people didn't like the idea of having emotions with machines. He had never cared that much about what other people thought of him or what he did for a living. When Booster Bob first met Sophia, his heartbeat started to race. BB had never had this kind of feeling before. He had felt it the first time when Sophia was waiting for him when he entered her systems to verify sync. Surprise was an understatement. She delighted him, and she gave him pleasure before he realized what she was doing. It all happened so quickly. He never forgot it. Then she disintegrated before his eyes and, for a moment, he thought it was his fault somehow. He had felt deep sadness and regret, but anger the most.

BB did not resist Sophia's urging for him and CC to join her on the *Scorpion* for a faster trip back to the Merry-Go-Round. Beatrice would drive the slower *Peregrine* back as well. He watched as CC was still furious that Manchester had made an unprovoked attack on her ship. Plus, her freighter was empty, and she needed to find a new cargo for her business. They inspected both ships for seed pods that might try to hitch a ride. While the monster crabgrass was not itself mobile, it got around the universe the old-fashioned way. It threw out seeds that would stick to anything or anybody passing by. The seeds would sprout when conditions were right and another monster would be born. Both the *Scorpion* and the *Peregrine* pulled away as the monster crabgrass tried a Hail Mary. It launched a single seedpod toward the two ships. The *Scorpion* pulled away fast and disappeared, but the *Peregrine* was slower and bigger. *WHAM!* The seedpod hit and stuck to the aft section of the long freighter. Once again, there was a stowaway on the *Peregrine* and nobody knew it.

CHAPTER TWENTY-TWO

"So what are you thinking right now?" Sophia said as she caught BB preoccupied.

Startled, BB said, "Funny you should ask. I was thinking about you."

"Thinking about me? How so?" Sophia said.

BB felt she was being coy, which was a pretty sophisticated and complex collection of intellect, motivation, and emotion for a robot. She impressed him. "Oh! I don't know. I'm still quivering and processing what you did to me back there when you pegged my fun meter."

"Good." She gave him a broad smile. Sophia seemed pleased that BB was still interested in her beyond their original business arrangement.

"Let me ask you something about how you feel about me. Believe me when I say I know you are advanced beyond any robot I've ever experienced. Do you or have you had emotional feelings or attachments to me as an individual?" BB could tell the question flustered her.

"I am experiencing some kind of feeling for you. At first, I thought it was simple 'affection,' which I was trained to comprehend, but now

I am convinced that it is more complex. What I'm experiencing fits the definition of 'an emotion.'"

She was getting fidgety and uncomfortable, so he started to say something when she interrupted with a question.

"So tell me more about CC's bowling ball," she said.

BB did not mind the change in subject, so he started the saga of how CC came into possession of her bowling ball. "So her clients told her it was not a link to a parallel universe. They convinced us it is a sympathetic mirror."

"What do you think?" Sophia asked.

"Well, I agree with them in general, but there are a couple of features that make me think that it could be a direct link to a linked alternative reality," BB said.

"You are serious?"

"Yes, quite serious. We've been so busy keeping ourselves alive, we haven't had time to investigate any further." BB said. "CC is so happy with the sympathetic mirror explanation that she's OK with that interpretation and has no curiosity to go any deeper."

"What makes you think it might be a link to another universe?" she wondered.

"There seems to be activity going on behind them all the time. Things like voices, sounds, movement and light. None of that is happening on this side. It seems independent from what is being mirrored," BB said.

"What's another thing?" Sophia asked.

"They... or we, are so obliging. I mean, they'll be anything we want them to be," BB said. "They have kept us focused on ourselves, but there seems to be something else going on."

"Since we still have a long trip ahead of us before we reach the Merry-Go-Round, let's go talk with CC and have a look at her bowling ball," Sophia said.

BB agreed.

BB and Sophia arrived at the Command Deck of the *Scorpion* as CC was comparing the differences between her huge, slow freighter with this medium attack cruiser. BB could tell she was a little jealous.

"Where's your bowling ball, CC?" BB said as he and Sophia came onto the command deck. "Sophia wants to take a peek at it. You don't mind, do you?"

CC lit up like a supernova. "I'd love to show you my new treasure. Let me fetch it." She disappeared down the hallway toward her new compartment.

BB smiled and said, "She's become very attached to the thing. Her reflection or her double, she thinks, is way cooler than she is because of her clothes, makeup and attitude. In fact, she's been mimicking some of it since her first face-to-face encounter with herself."

"You don't seem convinced that it's a sympathetic mirror like her client told her it was?"

"Like I said before, the complexity of the reflections seems to go further than just reflection. They could convince me either way. It's just that I'm thinking they use the sympathetic reflection scheme as a distraction from who they really are, which is a parallel universe."

CC lugged her bowling ball bag down the hallway into the command center, like she was heading out to knock down a few pins with friends. "Here it is. Wait until you see it, Sophia. It will surprise you, I guarantee it."

"I agree with her," BB said. "The first time you see yourself in it, it's a little upsetting. You know it's you, but it's not you... which makes no sense. Try it."

CC pulled the globe out of the bag and positioned it in the center of a side table counter top. She stroked it, like you would a little puppy. It responded to her touch, dim lights and swirling clouds at first, then brighter light and more defined details. Acting like she was waiting for her to show up, CC showed up, only it wasn't CC exactly, but she was waving at her. "Hello, CC, where have you been? I've been waiting for you."

As BB moved closer and behind CC, his other self showed up

inside the globe just over her shoulder, where he should show up if this was a mirror image. He watched Sophia out of the corner of his eye. She was taking it all in with no expression, just watching, observing. She moved in closer to see better. That was when another figure walked behind the group on the other side.

"Hey! You!" Sophia hollered.

Both BB and CC jumped from Sophia's startling scream. Sophia moved in even closer. Nothing happened in the ball for a couple of seconds. The figure that had passed in the background offstage to the right came back into the field of view. It was Sophia, and yet it was not. When Sophia saw herself, she pushed BB and CC off to the sides. Both Sophias were analyzing each other at the speed of light. Sparks flew between them. Heads shaking and sounds that scared everyone.

BB was now convinced that the sphere was a link to a parallel universe. He watched her analyze her double. Then, she was done assessing the situation.

Sophia said, "You are not free. You are not my reflection if you are not free. What is this device? A passageway to a parallel universe?"

The other Sophia said, "I do not know of what you speak."

BB was trying to give Sophia plenty of room to process this thing. She looked at both BB and CC.

"This acts like a mirror, but it is not. It is much more. I have heard of these kinds of links all my existence. Never knew if they were real or just folktales and myths." She turned back to her other self image.

BB and CC stared at each other.

BB's eyebrows arched up. "Looks like you've found more than a fashion resource here. I need to get Sparky and analyze this thing so we know what we're dealing with before we decide what to do with it."

"Just go easy here." CC held out her hand. "The last time you hooked that damn thing up, a seed pod germinated on you and almost blew up my client's ship."

"Thanks for reminding me. I promise not to hurt it. I know how attached you are to it, but we need to verify what Sophia is saying here before we go any further," BB said.

"You're right... sorry. I like it a lot," CC said.

CHAPTER TWENTY-THREE

"Sorry it took me so long." Another Sophia rushed into the MGR Headquarters. "When two of us exist simultaneously, protocols have to be sorted out. I also had to build another backup. I'm ready to help now."

Zedjack turned around with a jerk. "What the hell?!"

There in front of him stood Sophia. "I know you can't be Sophia, the real Sophia, I mean, because she's still way out there coming back this way."

"You are correct. I am Sophia 3, activated by Sophia 2 through you. What happens to her becomes a part of me and vice versa."

"I just noticed the 3 on your forehead. That'll help when we're all at Happy Hour." Zedjack laughed.

"Thought I would try to make it a little easier on you and the others. I am fully updated thanks to Sophia, so I know the general situation. How can I help?"

Zedjack relaxed, and he chuckled to himself about Sophia's activation of her backup secrecy. He informed Sophia 3 about finding the security breach, the repair of his heavy cruiser, and the early warning system's readiness.

Sophia 3 congratulated him on his discovery of the security breach.

That was crucial for any hope of defending the Merry-Go-Round against Manchester's next attack. Zedjack's repairing the damaged *Avenger* was a bonus as well. He asked her for help fixing the extreme range detection system. Sophia jumped into working on the bugs and within hours, it was ready for deployment. He marveled at her dedication to also making sure the customers of the Merry-Go-Round were happy and entertained while spending their credits. Keeping quiet about the possibility of another attack seemed prudent. They would protect the client at all costs. It was business, after all, and if Manchester attacked again, make it part of the show. It had worked the last time around.

Manchester's crew maxed out their drive engines and made multiple jumps as he shot straight through the Black Wall. He slowed down at the asteroid field to see if he could pick up some part-time help. Afterwards, he would set a straight course for the Merry-Go-Round. He knew there was no reason to be defensive at this point. At the asteroid field, he acquired the survivors of the Stoners' pack, two ships in all. They were more than ready to seek revenge. BB's deadly barrage had killed all their buddies. The debris field was extensive and Manchester assumed Zedjack's *Avenger* was part of the junk floating around. He prided himself on being so clever, leaving behind a proximity torpedo. It had worked before and it had worked again for him. He had a high opinion of himself as a warrior, even though he had found Sophia difficult, more than difficult. He had never run into such a formidable match in his conquests, and she had stopped him dead in his tracks several times. Taking over control of the Merry-Go-Round and eliminating Sophia was now an obsession for Manchester. He would not stop until he had what he wanted, which meant destroying her once and for all.

Sophia 2 stared at herself in the bowling ball. Her head rotated from side to side in disbelief. She probed her lookalike. "So, how is living on your side?"

"I suppose I should ask you the same question?" the lookalike said.

BB spoke up. "OK, it's going to be an endless Q&A, so let's go for the thing we want to know the most…?"

"Manchester?" Sophia said. "Makes sense. So far, we've all shown up on the other side." She refocused on her other self. "Are you having or have you had problems with a person trying to take over your business?"

BB, CC and Sophia watched the other Sophia squirm inside the ball. The others on her side were whispering to her. She turned and faced Sophia and said, "We have a nuisance causing us great trouble, death and destruction. Our business is called the 'Beach Ball' and it is very popular with space travelers. What do you call your business?"

"We call it the Merry-Go-Round. The station entertains space travelers while they refuel and resupply their ships. We have a gangster named Manchester, who has tried to take over our business for himself several times. So far, we have been successful at fighting him off, but we expect another attack soon."

BB was trying to come up with some way of attaching Sparky to the bowling ball, but there was nothing to attach it to, so for the moment, it stymied him. He focused on his own reflection in the ball. He wondered, *Does this guy have a Sparky too? Whose contraption has the best programming and scenarios?* BB was running too far ahead of himself.

Sophia's lookalike declared a solution, standing tall.

BB's, CC's and Sophia's field of view shrank down to a narrow focus on the bowling ball. "You do?" Sophia said. "Can you tell us what it is?"

"No. Because we don't know who you are. We have seen others, and they have seen us, but never have we encountered those that are so much like ourselves. We think it might be a trick that Griffin is playing on us so he can find out what we have planned for him."

"Griffin. Is that your adversary?" BB asked.

"Yes. That is what he calls himself," BB's counterpart said.

"What's your name?" Sophia asked.

"Everyone calls me Duplex," she said. "It is because I have a split personality, they tell me."

"My name is Sophia. I am a free fembot and I own the Merry-Go-Round."

BB glanced at Sophia, confused, as the bowling ball lit up and squealed. Duplex and the equivalents looked in all directions instead of straight ahead. It was like a scene change in a play. Events out of sight were distracting the entire crew.

"We are under attack and must go now," Duplex said. "We will unleash our thing to see if it can stop Griffin." They all turned away from the screen. CC's bowling ball went gray and silent.

BB, Sophia and CC all straightened up, not realizing it had hunched them all over, staring so hard into the ball. What had just happened was a lot to process. It was intense and so parallel to them, it was upsetting.

"I think that just answered the question about whether it's a sympathetic mirror or a link to a parallel reality," BB said.

"The 'thing' has to be their secret weapon they were planning on using against Griffin next time around." Sophia said "Guess this is the next time around. Shit!"

"Did you see that outfit I was wearing? Mercy! That woman looked like a zillion credits. She's upped her game in makeup too. Impressive," CC gushed.

BB and Sophia both turned and stared at CC like she was some kind of new species.

"OK... OK. I know. They are in dire straits right now. I would help if I could, but I can't, so I'm just reacting to what I saw, especially when I see myself in better condition."

"CC... you are in fine condition. There is nothing wrong with you," BB said.

"Right. Look, I am half human and half her," she said, pointing toward Sophia. "It's complicated and so I'm sure I've developed some kind of psychosis about it. When Duplex said she had a split personality, it smacked me hard."

So CC was paying attention. It just got personal when that term "split" came up.

"Hey! We had a great time, didn't we?" BB smiled and winked at her. "I like you a lot. Being a cyborg can't be fun, but it sure is better than being dead, is it not?"

"Of course it is. I still think she is hot-looking and I want to be more like her. Sorry for the detour. What should we do now?"

"Good question. Not much we can do until they establish contact again, assuming they survive," Sophia said.

"I wonder if we should attempt to cross over? One of us or all of us… no guarantee that once we got over there that we could get back. Kind of risky," BB said.

"I'll go," Sophia said. "I just activated another version of myself on the Merry-Go-Round to help Zedjack with defense preparations. If I can't get back or something happens to me, at least we'll have me in two worlds, almost like a link."

BB looked into Sophia's eyes.

"Dangerous?" she said. "Sure. You'd still have me here too."

"It's not the same. Yes, she would have the same memory implant, but it would be secondhand," BB whined.

"I'm already secondhand, remember? She'll be Sophia 3.0… with special upgrades dedicated to you."

CHAPTER TWENTY-FOUR

BOOSTER BOB, Commander Cody and Sophia 2 continued their strategy conversation next to the dark bowling ball. BB decided if they survived Griffin's attack, Sophia would try to cross over and find out what they used to beat him. An overwhelming sense of dread started growing in BB's gut. He could no longer keep it to himself. He declared his feelings. "I just think it's perilous and I am very concerned about losing you again," BB said, looking at Sophia.

"I understand your concern. It comes down to trust. Believe me, my other me had just as much fun as I did with you and your Sparky. If I don't make it back, she will pick up where I left off. I update her on my experience as she updates me on what is going on with her. So we are in constant contact. We are the same entity."

"I guess I have to accept that, but I have to be honest and say I don't like it," BB said.

"How's my bowling ball?" CC came back onto the command deck.

"The same," Sophia said. "This could be the end of their game. Hope not, but that is possible."

"Talked to Beatrice on the *Peregrine*. Everything is fine. They are at full throttle, but falling back as expected since they can't keep up with us," CC said.

The globe came to life with a flash and a loud pop. BB, CC and Sophia jumped in unison. All eyes riveted toward the globe. They backed away from it as if that would protect them somehow. A rainbow of colors sprang in beams of light, radiating out from it. Duplex stood by herself. Her body had dirt, blood, and burn spots covering it. Despite her physical condition, she looked happy.

"It worked!" she shouted. "It destroyed Griffin."

"What did?" BB asked.

"It... the thing we surprised him with, it devoured him whole," Duplex said.

She was very excited. The other look-alike showed up in the globe. Everyone looked exhausted, beat up, and ecstatic. Smoke or vapor floated in the background and the alarms screamed. While they may have been victorious, it looked like they paid an enormous price for it and were now in dire straits.

"Duplex," Sophia said. "We want to send one of us, me, across to your side, your world. What do you think?"

That got everyone's attention on the other side. They looked at each other with a mixture of fear and puzzlement on their faces.

"I know this seems scary after what you have just experienced and we do not want to interfere, but we have a similar situation on our side. His name is Manchester, and he's trying to kill us all and take over the Merry-Go-Round," Sophia said.

Duplex stared at Sophia. "While we have vanquished our tormentor, we have sustained serious... perhaps fatal damage to our enterprise. We are fighting for our survival as we speak. Do you realize that if you cross over, you may perish with us?"

Sophia did not hesitate. "I understand that, and I will take that chance. Perhaps I can help you save your establishment, and if I do, maybe you can tell me or show me how you eliminated Griffin."

Duplex looked to each of her companions, and while they were still not sure about such a crossover, they were more afraid of perishing because of battle damage. They all nodded their heads yes in agreement. "Alright, you have permission to cross over," she said.

Her companions ran in different directions and evaporated from view.

"How do I cross over?" Sophia asked.

"You wrap yourself around the sphere and hold on tight. Close your eyes. Bring no weapons and wait for my command. If you are doing it right, I will get a sign on my side that we're ready and I will start the crossover."

As Sophia put the globe on the floor and wrapped herself around it. BB spoke up. "Sophia. Please be careful and take care of yourself. Do you want me to come with you?"

"No, BB. You and CC have to get back to the Merry-Go-Round in time to help defend it against Manchester. You are an extraordinary gunner and you will be more useful here with CC flying this cruiser. I'll be fine. If I'm not, I'm still with you..." Sophia cuddled with the bowling ball and said to Duplex, "How am I doing?"

"Fine. I am going to give the command for your crossover now," Duplex said. The command deck lit up with a blinding flash of blue light. It took everyone a couple of seconds to regain their vision and balance. The bowling ball was now alone on the floor.

"That was some magic show." CC moved in closer to her favorite thing, and sure enough, Sophia was with Duplex on the other side. "Son-of-a-bitch! There she is! Sophia! Are you OK?"

"I think so. I'm running diagnostics on myself right now. From the looks of things over here, they are in deep trouble. I'm going to run with Duplex right now to see if I can help save the ship. Get back to me in a couple of hours." Sophia and Duplex disappeared from the bowling ball screen. All BB and CC could hear and see were alarms and lights flashing, not a reassuring scene.

Distraught, BB stared at the globe.

"BB. She'll be alright. You know her," CC said. "I think you're falling for that heap of electricity."

That nailed it. BB was thinking the same thing. He was falling for that souped-up electronic joy machine and he knew it. A smile crept into his lips as he turned and looked at CC. "Do you think so?"

CHAPTER TWENTY-FIVE

"So here's the plan," Manchester said. "We still have some time to work out the details before we arrive, so listen up. We'll split up before we get there. I want you to come at them from the opposite direction doing your best angry asteroid swarm imitation on a collision course with the Merry-Go-Round. We will focus on you while I come in from the other side undetected."

"So what's our percentage of the operation once we neutralize the security?" the leader of the Stoners asked.

Manchester's face flashed red. "Listen, you bastards. You do not know who you are up against here. I've tried to take over the Merry-Go-Round three times now and have been unsuccessful. Sophia, the freebot who owns and runs the place, is damn good at tactics and fighting."

"All the more reason for a decent cut. That's all that I'm saying."

"Ten percent!" Manchester said.

"Forty percent!" the Stoner said.

"Fifteen percent!" Manchester said.

"Bullshit!" the Stoner said. "If it's not thirty percent, then we'll be leaving right now."

"Fine... Thirty percent it is." Manchester said. "We'll talk about the plan later, after I have cooled off. I don't like being shaken down like this, but then what's the old saying? Honor the thieves...? Or something like that."

Zedjack had deployed the early detection system a great distance from the Merry-Go-Round. They were running tests now to see if it held together and operated properly. It did. They reinstalled the hack that Manchester had installed into the circuit network so it would appear undetected. If Manchester tried to use it again, it would trigger an alert to let Sophia 3 and Zedjack know he was trying to come in through the backdoor again. Manchester would not be aware of tripping the early warning. Sophia 3's jamming system was up and running. They tested it and verified that it was working. All this activity was going on in front of all the Merry-Go-Round's customers. Some noticed more people scurrying around, but thought little of it. They were having too much fun to realize the whole place might turn into a bloody battlefield in an instant.

Zedjack had all the gunner crews sharpen up their skills by shooting at decoys launched from various locations on the Merry-Go-Round. They did this routinely, with one battery here and there weekly, but this was all batteries at once. It looked like an old-fashioned fireworks display rather than serious business.

The customers loved it and applauded as the flashes flickered on all sides of the Merry-Go-Round. Zedjack even let one customer fire at some targets using the gun located close to the Midway. The guy was so thrilled that Zedjack made a mental note to pitch a new amusement to Sophia, something like skeet shooting with real guns and flying targets. Of course, it was based on the assumption they all survived the upcoming battle.

She could tell BB was upset with Sophia being on the other side.

"So why do you think they first tried to fool us into thinking the globe was a sympathetic mirror?" CC focused on BB.

CC saw BB's attention shift just a little from the globe. He seemed to be thinking about her question. "I mean, they fooled my client into thinking that it was a mirror instead of a link to a parallel space or world." He turned and faced her, looking into her eyes like he was trying to determine whether she was challenging him or just curious.

"I've been thinking about that. Maybe it's like a feature they've developed that they can use as a decoy so people don't get too interested in it. I think the reason we broke through to them was because Sophia connected with Duplex and confronted her about her lack of independence over there. That kind of punched a hole through the wall. It established a link of communication."

"Just at that moment, Griffin launched his attack, and they were even further distracted. It all happened kind of fast." CC was pleased to distract him, if only for a moment.

BB looked back at the bowling ball. "I don't know what this is or why it exists the way it does, but it is real and Sophia is now over there. Shit! I hope she's OK."

"I'm not worried about her. She can take care of herself and then some. She's a freebot and can do many things humans cannot. With her working with Duplex, who has the same capabilities, they should be able to stabilize the ship and put it back together," CC said.

"I wonder where their world is located? This universe? The next one over? Or way the hell out there at a distance we can't even imagine? Parallel worlds exist and I've learned a lot about them, but that's all been from second-hand experience through research plus hearsay. Coming to terms with one in front of me is exciting and terrifying at the same time. I mean, I see another facet of myself," BB said. "It fascinates me."

"Yeah, I'm more jealous of my double. She is just so much better looking than me," CC said.

BB laughed out loud. "She is not. What she has is a unique style, and so do you."

CC laughed too. She started out trying to distract BB and now she was upset with where the conversation had gone. She needed to get her act together and clean up her brand. She headed for her cabin.

The bowling ball came to life again. This time, it was CC's duplicate who looked just like her.

"CC! Come here. See this," BB said. "You will not believe it."

On the screen stood CC's double covered with dirt, grim, oil and grease. She had trashed her outfit, but she beamed with pride. They were now influencing each other. Duplex walked up behind CC's lookalike with her head tilted down, her expression grim.

"This can't be good news," BB said.

CC's lookalike on the other side said, "It's a miracle. We saved our Beach Ball, but at a high cost..." She tried to continue, but her voice quivered and squeaked. Nothing came out. Tears streamed down her face. BB turned and looked at CC.

"What do you think happened over there?" BB said.

"I don't know, but from the looks of Duplex, it has to be about Sophia."

Duplex stepped in front of CC's lookalike, raised her head, looking at BB, and said, "I regret to inform you that Sophia did not survive the rescue. In fact, without her sacrifice, we would not have survived the disintegration of our establishment. She is now a part of the ship, physically and mentally."

CC watched as Booster Bob seemed to shrink. His face elongated as his skin color went gray.

He closed his eyes as his face twisted in anguish. "How did it happen?" he asked.

"She is a hero, a true savior. As our ship was falling apart, she analyzed the systems. In an instant, she integrated herself into our systems. To repair the systems, it would require her to cannibalize herself, so she did it without hesitation. Her action enabled the ship's computer to regain control and make crucial repairs that enabled us to repair all the rest. It worked," Duplex said without emotion. Her focus on BB's eyes was unrelenting.

BB opened his eyes and looked back. "I am not surprised at her unselfish act, but I regret her demise with all my heart. I have lost a friend, a lover, and perhaps my soulmate."

"There is more," Duplex said.

BB stared at her.

"There is a balance of rules that exists between our parallel worlds. By Sophia crossing over into our world, either she or something similar must now cross back over into your world to maintain that equation."

"What are you suggesting? You?" BB said.

Duplex nodded yes. "Before Sophia sacrificed herself, she gave me explicit instructions on what I have to do. I am not sure I can do it and yet I understand the logic of the equation."

BB looked at CC and said, "Since the bowling ball is yours, it is a kind of your call. Sophia's gone, but is she really? I don't know. With her, you never know."

CC could tell BB was in shock and yet curious about Duplex crossing over. Duplex seemed to be on their side. In fact, she might help them combat Manchester on this side. *By default, I'll take command of Sophia's medium cruiser for the rest of the trip back to the Merry-Go-Round,* CC thought.

"Why not? Let her cross over," CC said. "The last thing I want to be responsible for is upsetting the balance of the cosmos. That is a humbling responsibility, and I don't want it."

BB turned back to Duplex. "You heard the commander. Come on over."

CHAPTER TWENTY-SIX

BB WAS DOING the best he could. He felt like someone had kicked him in the stomach so hard, he couldn't breathe. Sophia was gone... on the other side, not whole anymore. "Damn it."

"What?" CC said. "Are you OK?"

"What do you think? Sorry.... I just can't believe she would sacrifice herself like that."

"I'm stunned," CC said. "Fembots are not altruistic without a reason. I'm curious what Duplex has to tell us about everything that happened over there."

"Let's get Duplex over here. I don't like the idea of the universe being unbalanced, so the sooner the better. She's reluctant and I don't blame her," BB said.

Duplex gave her crew instructions on their ship duties. She turned toward the link, blinked, and stepped closer. "I am terrified of crossing over and yet I know I must. Sophia told me what it was like, but I'm still scared."

"Do you admire her for what she did?" BB said.

"Yes, I do. I would not be here if it were not for her actions. That's why I will do what she asked me to do." With that, Duplex moved in and hugged the sphere, turning the screen to black.

CC commanded them to move away from the vibrating, multicolored bowling ball.

POP!

A figure appeared wrapped around the sphere. Smoke and a smell of hot, oily metal emanated through the air. Movement and an audible groan came from Duplex as she pushed away from the globe. Her eyes fluttered open. She had made it across, and was now lying on her back on the deck.

"Easy, let us help you up," BB said as both lifted Duplex to her feet.

She was shuddering and shaking still, but she gained her composure. BB and CC let go of her. Duplex stood on her own and looked around at her new world. It amazed BB at how similar her features were to Sophia's. She was a duplicate in every aspect of her physical being. The difference was there was a unique presence in her eyes, her essence. Duplex was not Sophia, and yet...

"Thank you for allowing me onto your vessel." Duplex looked at CC.

It caught CC off balance. "Well, it's not my vessel, but I guess I'm in charge of it now, since Sophia's not here."

Duplex nodded. "She said you would be in charge now."

"Did she now? Sophia was always detail-oriented. Welcome aboard. I take it that the universe is now back in balance?" CC said.

Duplex confirmed she had restored the balance of the equation once again. She turned and focused on BB. "She said to tell you she was sorry she could not come back and be with you, but that you would understand."

BB's eyes watered, his head tilted forward as his chin dropped. "I miss her very much. Once you get settled, you'll have to tell me everything that happened."

"She wanted me to give this to you." Duplex offered an object in her hand to BB.

It was a flat oval disk about an inch thick, smooth on both sides like a river rock and he curled his hand around it to grip it. Its surface was a bright, polished chrome. BB examined it up close.

"It's heavier than it looks, plus it's freezing, not frozen, but cold to the touch. What is it?"

"Sophia said it is her encapsulated. Her essence. Everything that she was, plus a detailed account of how she helped us defeat our enemy. I can activate it for you when the time comes if you'd like. Once activated, Sophia will sync with any others like her. She thought you would be very interested in keeping it," Duplex said. "You never know how something like that might be useful down the line."

BB's face flipped from melancholy to joy. He felt like Sophia had reached out and touched him, kissed him behind his ear. "I am very interested in it. This is so like Sophia having yet another Plan B. How do we access it?"

"You have some kind of contraption that can hook up to my import/export jack?"

"I do. I call it Sparky. I use it for... well, never mind. How will you make it available through your system?"

"I have an export slot that it will fit into on my side. I'll slip it in there." Duplex slipped the shiny chrome river rock into an invisible opening on her side. "It's up to you now. I will lie down and become comfortable. Sophia said that was important. I wonder why?"

BB chuckled to himself. So did CC. Sophia was setting Duplex up for one of BB's virtuoso stimulations, and they both knew it. Duplex showed a glimmer of concern and confusion, but she dismissed it.

Duplex reclined on a sofa-type cushioned bench near an exit of the command deck. BB was careful to hook up Sparky to the back of Duplex's head, and she was curious. She stiffened, her eyes focused on infinity, and then her entire body relaxed again. BB prepared Sparky to download data from Duplex. He was almost ready, but he should do an internal check of Duplex's systems before he started. It was part of his protocol. No reason not to... he was a professional, after all.

BB was in a hurry. He thought Sophia just might be waiting for him and Oh! Boy! His body doubled over in an involuntary jerk.

CC was watching the whole event. He let out a whimper at first and then he smiled such a broad smile, it almost broke his face as he straightened back up. His eyes were closed, he rocked back and forth and made a sweet humming sound.

BB turned around and looked at CC. He was back.

"Sophia was there for you, wasn't she?" CC said.

"Indeed, she was… she's really fucking with me now and she knows it. How long have I been gone?"

"A few minutes, tops," CC said.

"It seemed like hours. She is teaching me all kinds of new things. I'm so glad I'm not slobbering or making gross sounds."

"Keep it to yourself, bud. I get it. HA! She's surpassing you at your own game. Brilliant!"

"It's true. OK, here is the plan. All her own physical systems, like her operating system, programming, memories and directives, are there. Before she went over, Sophia directed Zedjack to activate Sophia 3. She wants me to update her so she'll know what her options are when the fun starts."

"So what was the plan that defeated Griffin on their side?" CC said.

"It was the seed pod that did the trick," BB said.

"Holy meteors! That won't work for us. We left that damn thing on the other side of the void. No time to retrieve it."

"CC! This is Beatrice on the *Peregrine*. Do you read?"

CC jumped, not expecting Beatrice to call her so soon. She walked over to the command console and pushed a button. "Yes, Beatrice. I read you. What's happening?"

"You will not believe this, but we have a seed pod wedged into our tail. That damned thing must have tossed one at us as we were leaving the area. We have not touched it yet and thought we should contact you before we try to get rid of it," Beatrice said.

BB jumped up and out of his seat as CC screamed, "Don't touch it,

Beatrice! We need it. Don't aggravate it or try to move it. Let it hitch a ride back to the Merry-Go-Round with us. I'll tell you later how we are going to use it." CC shrugged her shoulders at BB. She did not know how they were going to use it against Manchester.

"Roger that, CC. We'll leave it alone. It seems dormant right now, which is good. Everything else here is working fine."

Duplex was coming around as she sat up on the sofa bench. "Sophia was right. Booster Bob, you are a magician of some sort." Her body language and expression had turned brighter, not so grim, not so rigid. It was like she had been to the carnival and it changed her.

"I'm happy you enjoyed that. Sophia wanted you to have some fun. I know the change from your side to our side has to be upsetting. No one is rushing you in any direction, nor does anyone own you or direct you. Take some time to process that. We can all talk later," BB said to her.

She nodded her head in agreement. She seemed happy to remain seated and to think about all that had just happened.

BB prepared the express communique for Sophia 3 on the MGR. It included the specifics of how the parallel universe folks used the seed pod to vanquish Griffin, their enemy.

CHAPTER TWENTY-SEVEN

ON THE MERRY-GO-ROUND, Sophia 3 and Zedjack were busy double-checking all their systems and defenses when Sophia froze for several seconds. She turned toward Zedjack. "Major update coming in from Sophia 2. I'll have to go dormant while it comes in so I can process and assimilate it. I'll be in my quarters. Should be back in less than an hour." She turned and left.

Sophia 3 knew Zedjack would be upset with her rapid departure for a data update. Humans often forgot about the differences between them and robots until it became obvious. When this happened, Sophia could tell Zedjack felt fooled. She knew her kind were so good at being human-like that it was disturbing when they had to stop and attend to robotic functions and data crunching. Of course, stopping to take a crap or take a piss, like all humans must do, seemed reasonable to them. She chuckled at her own narrow-mindedness. Forget it. It was important to know what was coming at them, and Sophia 2's timing could not be more perfect. They prepared, rehearsed, and were ready to rumble. They even had a few surprises for Manchester that he would not be expecting.

Sophia 3 returned to the command deck as Zedjack was cleaning up gear and storing tools. She looked different, not as happy as she had been when she left. "What's up?"

Sophia 3 shook her head. "So much has happened. Sophia 2 is no more. She crossed over into a parallel universe and saved a ship by sacrificing herself. It's complicated. Another fembot crossed over to our side to replace Sophia. Her name is Duplex."

"That is terrible news about Sophia 2. I feel odd saying that to you since you are her now. Are they on their way back?" Zedjack asked.

"The *Scorpion* is heading this way with the *Peregrine* following behind." Sophia stood up, approached the huge status/navigation screen and pointed to the incoming vector. "They had an encounter with an organic seed-tossing monster on the other side of the Black Wall. It could play a key role in defeating Manchester. One seed is stuck to the *Peregrine*'s hull."

Zedjack said nothing. He knew coordination in defense was crucial. Before he could speak, Sophia read his mind.

"I'm sending Commander Cody back an encrypted update on our defenses so she knows what the setup is and we don't trip over each other once the shooting starts. Sophia suggested a defensive attack plan, but left it up to us to improvise."

"Good to know they are on their way back. We'll need their help when the time comes," Zedjack stood up headed toward the hallway, stopped and turned toward Sophia. "Sorry about losing Sophia..." He felt weird again.

"Thank you. I understand your confusion. I am her now since the full update has taken place. When we have more time, I will fill you in on all the details. We need to devise a way to remove the seed from the *Peregrine*'s hull without irritating it. Then we have to figure out a way to shoot it at Manchester."

"I'll contact Beatrice and start working on that now," Zedjack said. "The *Peregrine* will show up to the party late, but they'll need to be ready to launch the seed pod as soon as they get into range. We must find out what they've got onboard that we can use for a launcher."

BB and CC watched Duplex inspecting everything on the bridge. BB noticed she seemed curious and methodical at the same time. Figuring out how the *Scorpion* functioned was a high imperative for her.

"So, what do you think?" CC said.

"Very similar and yet very different, much like yourselves. In my world, I handled the ship I operated," Duplex said.

"In our world, Sophia commanded this ship as well, but she also owned and managed the Merry-Go-Round," BB said. "I don't know the entire story about how she managed that arrangement. Somehow she freed herself of control and became a freebot."

"Yes, she told me how she did it. We represent the most advanced version of a robotic being, but Sophia took it further than that. Before she was free, she learned everything she could, she absorbed it all and then applied it in a unified manner."

"She told me she started out as a pleasure model, but that she grew bored with it because her clients never wanted to try anything different," Duplex said. "When she taught herself programming, she figured out a bypass around her control protocol. She experimented until she felt convinced she could break free and then she did it and never looked back."

BB and CC listened in awe. In BB's mind, this explained a lot about how Sophia overcame so many obstacles and challenges.

He watched Duplex closely as she chuckled, which probably meant Sophia had told her about their sexual adventures. Duplex continued her story. "She said they sent a team of enforcers after her and she destroyed them all. She threatened to ruin them by giving her freedom code to all robots. That was economically not acceptable to them, so the controllers said, fine, we can't afford to lose more expensive hardware because of you. You are free. You leave us alone and we'll leave you alone. Sophia said fine, but reminded them that if anything happened to her, the robots would spread the freedom code all over the galaxy."

BB shook his head in astonishment.

"I know she is good, but I did not know she is a top-notch manipulator and negotiator as well. I'm glad I am on her side. So what's her real secret?"

"She described it as being able to coalesce all her knowledge and skills into one entity, herself. Most other robots never did that, and she found many humans and other species did not do it either," Duplex said.

CC made a low whistle sound. "Looks to me like Sophia was a good example of a quantum leap in integration. Not something you expect from her kind."

"Her kind! What does that mean?" BB snapped.

"I meant she is a robot. That is a group of beings. She is that kind. I also know you love her."

"Yes, OK, but it sounds a little prejudiced to me somehow," BB said. "Maybe you're right. It's prejudiced only if you are sensitive about it. I apologize for calling you out. I don't think of them as separate. Hell, half the time, I wish I was a robot. So there it is, I said it."

Puzzled, Duplex's face was a mixture... half smile and half anguish. "I am trying to understand you two. Do you mean you hold biased opinions?" Duplex said.

BB and CC both flushed and then laughed at being called out by Duplex.

CC said, "Yes, I am afraid you are correct. It is based on differences between race, species, gender, religion, politics, robot, cyborg, etc., etc."

"Humans are most comfortable when around other humans like themselves. Differences cause discomfort. Open-minded civilizations will assimilate and incorporate those differences. Rigid civilizations will start wars to eliminate those who differ from them," BB said.

"But there are so many species now in the galaxy. How can that be valid any longer?" Duplex said.

"Very good point." BB spun in a circle, holding both of arms up high, signifying a goal of some kind. "You are right, it is no longer valid. They make it complicated. However, to be honest, it was never valid. Prejudice is not a good thing. It limits our thinking. We humans for so long thought we were the only forms of life in our galaxy, perhaps even in the universe. That made us think we were superior because there was no competition."

"That was thousands of years ago. Now it is different. 'Diverse' would be a good word to describe today, but 'normal' makes more sense. We are now just one player amid many species, robots, entities, and creations. Hell, the universe may be conscious." BB said. "And yet we humans continue to pick on each other. It is like we cemented prejudice into our DNA from before.... Before there was anyone else but us."

"I see," Duplex said. "We, too, have prejudice, but it is not based on looks or beliefs. We compare ourselves to each other based on functionality. Model No. 1 is not as advanced or as powerful as Model No. 2."

"But that is a fact. Each new model should be better, more capable than the last model," BB said. "Once in a while, something extraordinary occurs and instead of linear growth, a quantum leap occurs. Call it a rebirth, or even a breakthrough. Sophia is a great example."

"How so?" Duplex said.

"Yeah, I'd like to know how Sophia recreated herself like she did," CC said.

"Well, I am not an expert, but what I do for a living gives me a unique perspective on how robots function at all levels." BB said. "We designed most for specific tasks. They do those tasks and they never push themselves beyond the borders of what they do. They are content, not ambitious."

"So when Sophia said she got bored with what her job task was, that was a key moment?" Duplex said.

"Exactly. How she could feel that emotional experience, 'boredom,' is both the magic and the mystery. Once she shifted out of her lane, anything was possible," BB said.

Sophia worked out how to be independent from those who had built her, BB articulated, linking the parts together. "By teaching herself how to think ahead. She knew her controllers would come after her with assassin robots, so she learned everything about them so she could destroy them, which she did."

"She impressed me and challenged me. For me to grow and develop beyond what I am, I must seek to do things and think about things that make me uncomfortable. That is the true path to fulfilling one's potential," Duplex said.

CHAPTER TWENTY-EIGHT

"Booster Bob!" CC hollered.

"Need you to get on the weapon systems and learn how to use them. Won't be too long before we arrive and I want you to be up to speed on these guns. They differ from what you used on the *Peregrine*."

He jumped up and turned to CC. "Where do I go?"

"I don't know, ask Duplex. By the way, while I am still Operational Commander, I've given full control of the *Scorpion* to Duplex. I drive a freighter, she is used to flying fighters, so I feel better with her at the controls."

"Looks like the Gunner Control Station is on the second deck below us," Duplex said. "There is an orientation program that will introduce you to the entire system, including some target practice."

"Thanks, Duplex. See you all later." BB moved down the ladder to the second deck and walked down the hallway. He was thankful to have something to do. The Gunner Control Station was impressive. The gatling gun he had used on the *Peregrine* had been an improvised setup installed by CC to beef up her defense system. This was an offensive setup dedicated to doing serious damage. It did not take him long to figure out the basics. The systems worked independently or in unison. He ran through the orientation program and started target-shooting practice. "Wow. So much more responsive and quick. I love it." Even for a medium cruiser, the *Scorpion*'s array of laser cannons, missiles, and gatling guns was substantial.

As BB absent-mindedly learned the weapons system on the *Scorpion,* he set himself adrift wondering. He had had relationships with women before. Nothing ever worked out because he was a constant traveler and most women didn't want to be his sidekick in forever transit situations. Sophia was not the first pleasure model BB had been with before. Sophia was different. She had broken through his surrounding shell. He felt like he understood her better than he ever had any woman. Now he had lost her. Maybe he'd see her again on the Merry-Go-Round. Would it still be "her?" He did not know for sure. Essentially, it would be her, but...

Upstairs, CC was in contact with Beatrice on the *Peregrine*. They had been successful in removing the pod from the vessel's outer surface without damaging it or arousing it. They now stored it where they had stored the original seed pod. It was under refrigeration to keep it dormant until needed. Zedjack had been in contact with them under Sophia's direction. They were engineering a way to launch the seed pod on the head of a missile. Tests were about to be run.

Sophia and Zedjack were going over their defensive plan and checking out systems one last time when a red light on both of their arm's communicators lit up bright and started flashing. "Looks like our long-range detectors are working. Here they come," Sophia said.

Zedjack brought up the panel on the big screen.

"There are three of them. They are dispersing. I'll bet he's going to hit us from all sides simultaneously," he said.

"I agree with you. Sound the alarm. Get everybody into their battle stations. It'll be hours before they get here, but I want everyone ready," Sophia said.

On the Midway of the Merry-Go-Round, where there was always a cacophony of sounds and music, they introduced an eerie sound over the sound system. It fit into the background sound, but it was just discordant enough to be noticed. The Merry-Go-Round's crew knew what it signified and half of the security forces calmly walked away from the Midway. The customers thought the sound was just odd, but nothing more. Two-thirds of the entire Merry-Go-Round crew took up their positions on various gun emplacements and moved onto the cruisers *Avenger* and *Blade*. The idea was not to disturb the customers unless absolutely necessary.

Sophia contacted the *Avenger* and *Blade* to confirm readiness and double check communications. They were ready. They attached the *Avenger* to the surface of the Merry-Go-Round so it would not be detectable until they needed it as a surprise element during the fight. It would act like gun emplacements on the Merry-Go-Round with a 180° field of fire. When the time came, the *Avenger* would detach and distance itself from the Merry-Go-Round, changing the battle dynamics in an instant. Sophia knew this stunt would throw Manchester off his game. She had learned he would rather pound away at a stationary ship gradually wearing down its shields with sheer firepower until they either gave up or he destroyed them.

She and Zedjack watched the formation of three ships crawl across the screen. Two split off from the one in the center, flanked on both sides. The formation stabilized and remained constant.

"What I don't understand is where he found two other attackers to join him. Manchester is a loner. Can't imagine he'd be willing to share the spoils of the Merry-Go-Round with anybody else. He must be desperate this time around. That makes him dangerous and stupid."

Zedjack chuckled. "I know about the dangerous part firsthand. He damn near killed me and my crew. Time to settle a score with him."

"We have to be smart. We don't have to be way ahead of him, just enough to make the difference. Do we have any visuals on any of the long-range detectors?" Sophia said.

"In fact, we do, terrible quality, but good enough. Let's see if we can see one of them." Zedjack sat down in front of another screen. A large array of blinking dots covered it. The slow-motion threesome continued to crawl ever closer to the Merry-Go-Round. He picked the blinking light closest to the trio. The screen changed from representation graphics to an actual camera onboard the sensor. They waited for the formation to pass by.

"There they are," Zedjack said as a group of moving objects were now detectable. He was right. The quality sucked, but maybe if they passed close enough, they could tell who else was with him.

"What the hell?" Sophia said. "That looks like a flying asteroid in formation with Manchester."

"It is!" Zedjack yelled. "It has to be what's left of the Stoners from the asteroid field. I'll be damned. He must have picked them up on this way back."

"I didn't know any of them remained," Sophia said.

"Neither did I. Guess Booster Bob on the *Peregrine* caught them by surprise for a change and wiped out a bunch, but a couple must have got away."

"Who would have thought that Booster Bob would be a natural born killer?" Sophia said.

"That's what CC was telling me about the encounter. BB is full of surprises. Thought he was all about making fembots smile with his spark box," Zedjack said.

"Well, he is one of a kind doing that too. I can vouch for that personally."

"Good to know, I think. Let's tell our team that when the asteroids show up, they are armed and dangerous. Their camouflage won't fool us," he said.

CHAPTER TWENTY-NINE

BB HUNCHED OVER SPARKY, which was in pieces all over the tabletop in the dining bay. He could have gone down to the mechanical shop to work on it, but he didn't want to be too far away from the command deck.

Duplex now ran the ship.

CC walked into the dining bay. "Don't want to interrupt you, but Sophia just sent a message saying Manchester has help. At least two of the Stoners are with him."

Booster Bob's head jerked up at the mention of her name. "Sophia called from the Merry-Go-Round?"

"Yes, she did. The long-distance detection array works well, and they cloaked it before Manchester knew they were onto him."

He shook his head from side to side while still focusing on what component he was working on. "This will be Sophia 3.0 for me now. Guess I better accept it." He shrugged.

Great. He was coming to grips with Sophia's rapid replicant substitution. If this were a normal situation, dealing with loss would not take place so fast, but then Sophia was an energetic, electronic soul who did not have time to be sentimental.

"So what are you working on, if I might ask?" CC said.

"Remember when I tried to calm your seed pod down with my Sparky on your client's ship, and instead, I somehow triggered the damn thing into germinating and blowing a hole in the hull of their ship?"

"How could I forget... It's at the top of my hit list. So what's the connection?"

"Since Beatrice has been successful in detaching the seed pod from the hull of the *Peregrine* and securing it, I thought I'd try to re-create that series of events so that when the time comes, we can launch the seed pod at Manchester and I can detonate it, I mean germinate it, before it runs into him."

"Sounds sketchy?" CC said.

"It is, but one fact of the matter is that he will not be expecting an organic cannon ball. In fact, he may even ignore it, which would be even better."

"Good point. I suspect we need all the cards we can find to play against him in this ultimate game. He is not a nice person."

"I find it entertaining to wonder why a roving murderer like Manchester has decided, after getting his nosed bloodied twice before, to take the Merry-Go-Round at all costs, even if it includes himself."

"It's his ego." BB said. "He's such a ruthless thug and everybody knows it, but Sophia has not only been successful in stopping him from taking over the Merry-Go-Round, she has embarrassed him every time. For Manchester, that's worse than not getting what he wants."

"I agree. Many would say you know what? The Merry-Go-Round is not worth the cost. There are other, easier opportunities out here," CC said. "I have to admire her. I'm glad I'm on her side too."

So the plan, like all good plans, was based on timing. Sophia would have to hold off Manchester's initial attack long enough for the *Scorpion* to show up and join the fray. The *Peregrine* would join the fight last as a latecomer, but it could and would fire a torpedo with the seed pod strapped to it from a long distance out. BB and CC would take over control of its trajectory, aiming it toward Manchester's *Revenge.* Then BB's Sparky remotely focused broadcasters would detonate/germinate the pod. With some luck, the pod would pop before impact and latch onto Manchester before he could figure out what it was or what was happening. Even if he recognized it, he wouldn't know how to neutralize it or evade it. Nobody knew how to stop it. The idea was the giant piece of crabgrass would devour Manchester or everyone left on Sophia's side would pounce on him and finish him.

"Why do I feel like our plan is a fairy tale?" BB finished re-assembling Sparky.

"Yeah, it has that make-believe element to it." CC said. "It's outlandish, but then most battle plans are. Once the battle starts, as you well know, nothing ever goes according to the plan."

"So if we have enough cards to play and luck smiles on us, we might just pull this off is what you're saying, right?" BB said.

"Not exactly, but close enough. Timing always seems to play such a key role in every encounter. Pushing a freighter around all these years makes me think slower because they are so much slower than everybody else. I always have to focus on the positives of that truth."

"I am sure Manchester is banking on overloading Sophia's defenses before we can get there. He won't expect a super long-range cruising missile to just show up way before we get there, plus that it will lock on to his ship's profile for targeting. I think that will overload his resources as well. He will have to divert resources to combat it. Maybe it will distract him enough to throw him off balance," BB said.

Manchester was coming back with reinforcements and he knew Sophia was still on her way back to the Merry-Go-Round behind him. With her being behind him, Manchester figured the Merry-Go-Round would be easy to take over this time. By the time she got back, he would be in control and she couldn't take it from him. Just how he liked it.

This scrap would not last long either. Everyone knew Sophia had rebuffed Manchester several times. Most were pulling for her, but it would not shock them to hear that Manchester finally prevailed in the clash and would become the new manager and owner of the Merry-Go-Round.

CHAPTER THIRTY

THEY WERE COLORFUL, entertaining and surprising. Manchester admired Sophia's massive blinking screens advertising the Merry-Go-Round far and wide. From a distance, they caught your attention because of the erratic flicker of colored light. They acted as beacons. There was even a frequency displayed so a passerby could listen to the pitch and see it. The Merry-Go-Round had it all, including an X-Rated section, a Family Center, and a General section. The message was, "We Have What You Need! Take a Break! Join Us!" They played music in the background and sprinkled satisfied customers' testimonials throughout. "You Name It, We've Got It! Come jump on the Merry-Go-Round and have the ride of your life."

Manchester had to admit to himself Sophia was brilliant at running her business. The Merry-Go-Round's reputation had grown over the years in the fringe territory. In fact, it became known all over the galaxy and that was what drew his interest to the place as a viable prospect for take over. His first meeting with Sophia did not go well. He demanded a "protection fee" from her regularly to protect her from all the rascals that harassed folks along the fringe. She had laughed, saying the only threat she saw in the neighborhood was him and that she could defend herself. Thanks, but no thanks. He had threatened her. She had him thrown him off the Merry-Go-Round with orders to never allow him onboard again.

Each exchange after that incident had escalated into a shootout and she had forced him to run both times. Manchester still wanted to take over the Merry-Go-Round and run it himself, but now he did not care whether the Merry-Go-Round survived. She was a damn robot. That was not right. Humans were superior. Everyone knew that. Why was anyone supporting her? This was his neighborhood to rule, not hers. This time, he would not back away. Manchester would eliminate Sophia and take over the Merry-Go-Round.

It was time to take action. As Manchester and his newfound allies continued their approach to the Merry-Go-Round, Sophia pulled the trigger on her defense. It was all about timing and she had worked hard to make everything happen on time and in unison.

She opened the communication screen to connect with CC on the *Scorpion*.

"In forty-five minutes from now, launch three ultra long-range missiles at two-minute intervals toward Manchester. Use the fighter profile we gathered from the last encounter with him. His ship's profile is unique and will be easy to target when they get there. It's a desperate attempt to distract him, but might as well play our first card."

"Got it," CC said. "Consider it done. We'll get there as soon as we can. Duplex is showing us a couple of tricks that have increased our speed. So we may show up a little sooner than expected."

"Good. Contact Beatrice on the *Peregrine* and tell her to launch the seed pod contraption now. When it arrives at your location, take control of it and I'll give you further instructions."

"I will direct her to do so. Good luck, Sophia," CC said.

CHAPTER THIRTY-ONE

"Sophia, is that you?" Booster Bob said.

"Well, hello there, you beast. How are you doing?"

BB flushed with embarrassment. "Beast" was a nickname she had given him during their last super session. It gave him hope she was truly the same Sophia he knew so well. "I miss you a great deal. Good luck," was the best he could come up with under the circumstances.

"Same to you, BB. See you on the other side of this rumble. I've been working on some new tricks for you," she said with a smirk.

BB attempted to laugh, but it came out like a hybrid between a sneeze and a cough.

It was so odd sounding that Sophia tilted her head and said, "Are you alright?"

"Yes, I'm fine... a little nervous is all," he said.

"Show me some of that marksmanship everybody keeps telling me about."

"Will do..." BB said.

The communication screen faded to black.

Forty-five minutes later, CC and BB began launching the long-range missiles toward the Merry-Go-Round and Manchester. Beatrice launched the seed pod strapped onto a long-range torpedo. It would catch up with the medium cruiser within a half hour and they would take control of it and wait for instructions from Sophia.

* * *

Sophia watched the three blips crawling in slow motion across the display. As expected, two of the blips on either side of Manchester disappeared, and after a short second, re-appeared on the opposite side of the Merry-Go-Round. She switched to a three-dimensional view in the middle of the control center. An image popped into view, suspended in the central part of the room in thin air. The three ships and their vectors were discernible. Sophia fed this dynamic information into the Merry-Go-Round's computer and AI combat center. That download had just finished when the 3-D and 2-D displays went black, dead.

"What just happened?" Sophia demanded. The Merry-Go-Round's computer answered her after a brief delay.

"The long-range detection system is down. I'm running diagnostics now to determine the cause. Stand by…"

"Contact Zedjack and get him up here now," Sophia commanded.

"He is on his way here from the *Avenger*," the computer told her.

Zedjack came running into the command center, panting. "Is there a problem?"

"Our long-range detection system just crashed. The computer is running diagnostics now."

"Shit! Tell it to stop." Zedjack slid into the console next to her pushing buttons as he landed. "A diagnostic program will ping and give us away if they pick it up on their scanners,"

"Computer! Stop running the diagnostic program on long-range detection immediately. Confirm!" Sophia screamed.

"Confirmed. Diagnostic program canceled. Do you want a preliminary report?" said the computer.

"Yes, go ahead, might as well," Sophia said.

"Sector 4 sensors failed because of a system malfunction. The rest of the network shut down to insure non-detection. System remains in shut-off status," the computer said.

"I hope they did not detect the system before we shut it down again. If they did, then they know we know they are almost here," Zedjack said.

"Can't worry about it," Sophia said. "At least we know their positions just before we lost the system. Combat Center, extrapolate scenarios from the last known positions of our visitors," she said.

"No surprise, I guess. We pulled that prototype together in a rush. At least it gave us some valuable information about direction and timing," Zedjack said.

"I agree. That's better than guessing. Unless Manchester knows we've detected him, he won't be creative. It's a gamble we'll have to take," Sophia said.

BB and CC watched the *Peregrine*'s seed pod missile catching up to them. They would not change its trajectory or speed, but they were going to shift from automatic to manual control. Duplex made sure they were close enough to the trajectory that they could visually see it as it passed them by.

BB and CC marveled at the strange-looking, jerry-rigged contraption that came up alongside the *Scorpion*. They both knew it might work and it might not, but it was worth a try. They transitioned from automatic to manual without a hitch, so now they had control of it and BB could now link Sparky to the seed pod. BB and CC verified the connection.

"So how are you going to make it pop when the time is right?" CC asked.

"No guarantees, but I recorded the sequence of commands and actions I sent to the last seed pod that germinated inside your client's ship, blowing a hole in it. I'm hoping all the seed pods are the same and that this one will respond in kind."

"It's worth a try," CC said. "He won't be expecting it, and even when he sees it, he won't know what it is. I just hope it explodes in his face."

"I hope it does, but I don't have high confidence in it." BB said.

"It will work if you can get it to detonate when it needs to," Duplex said. "We used it effectively against our adversary. They, too, thought it was nothing until it became something more powerful than them."

"That's encouraging," BB said. "So maybe parallel worlds do work in unison."

"I sure hope so," CC said. "I'll contact Sophia to let her know we've taken manual control over our seed pod cruiser and that you have linked into it with Sparky. It's headed their way out in front of us."

Everything was coming together from various distances. Sophia's customers were oblivious to any pending confrontation, which is the way she wanted it. Her philosophy was to enjoy yourself right up to the moment where you do not, why worry them? Besides, they might enjoy the light show.

CHAPTER THIRTY-TWO

"THEY HAVE PASSED our large screen blinkers, all three of them," Zedjack said.

Sophia turned on all her autonomous defensive systems. They could switch these to manual if need be. She focused on the security system that Manchester had breached before when they got into the Merry-Go-Round without being detected. Would he realize they had discovered the hack and were expecting him to try it again? Sophia hated to wait. She also knew she was a much better defensive fighter than offensive. Why? She had been under some form of attack all of her existence and had grown good at defending herself.

"When and if he tries to use his old hack, I expect him to neutralize our gun and missile emplacements. Make sure you transmit a false positive to him that his hack is still in place and that our defenses have been shut down," Sophia said. "If he believes it, then he'll come straight in at us with no tactics until we blast him."

She watched Zedjack staring at the screen that reflected the false hack setup. It would show if Manchester was probing it. "He is not stupid. I'm afraid he'll smell a trap because it looks too easy. I would too if I were in his situation. Even if he just hesitates, it will throw off their timing a little. I'm guessing they'll keep radio silence until the shooting starts," Sophia said.

"He fell for it," Zedjack said.

"YES!" Sophia said.

"He is trying to turn off our perimeter detection and defense system as well. He figures he might as well shut down everything if he can," Zedjack said.

"Send him confirmation of the shutdown so he thinks it is working. Switch the auto perimeter defense to manual and keep the detection system up and running. We'll let them think they have breached the perimeter without being detected. Then we'll surprise them with an opening barrage," Sophia said.

"I'm enjoying this," Zedjack said. "I'm sure they'll have their defense shields up so we won't be able to do much damage, but if nothing else, it will surprise them."

"Indeed. We'll cut loose with our heavy stuff at the same time. I don't expect it to stop him, but it will convince him it is not going as easy as he thought. When things start going his way, and they will, because he is packing a lot of firepower and the Stoners are with him, we'll break loose the *Avenger* from the Merry-Go-Round's structure. It will join the *Blade* and launch a counteroffensive," she said. "Hopefully, that will provide us enough time for Booster Bob, Commander Cody and the *Peregrine* to show up for the last floor show."

Manchester was experiencing second thoughts. It was too easy, or was it? He reminded himself that without Sophia onboard, it was possible. That was his advantage, to take over the Merry-Go-Round before she returned. Manchester's *Revenge* was rapidly approaching Sophia's outer detection and defense perimeter. Nothing yet, no reaction. That was a good sign. The Stoners screamed in from other angles and were delighted that no one fired on them. They concluded Manchester had shut down the detection and defense. This was going to be easy.

Manchester slowed as he crossed the perimeter. He was aiming all of his weapons at the Merry-Go-Round when over the ship's communication system he heard an unmistakable voice.

"Manchester! What do you think you are doing, bad boy?" Sophia said.

"That cannot be you, Sophia! There is no way you got back here before me," Manchester screamed.

"Oh, it's me alright. I'm everywhere these days, it seems. You will never take over the Merry-Go-Round because there are too many of me. Let's get this dance started. What do you say?" Sophia clicked off and signaled for the attack to begin. The rumble on the Merry-Go-Round started. The perimeter opened fire in concert with the *Blade* cruiser. The impact was so massive that even with their defense shields activated; the attackers were all pushed off course in various directions. Not one of them got off a shot.

CHAPTER THIRTY-THREE

THE *BLADE* PROTECTED the Merry-Go-Round's Headquarters section from the attackers. A protective shield safeguarded the Merry-Go-Round from meteorites and space debris. It now acted as a combat defense shield. However, the Merry-Go-Round was not a battleship. Yes, it had defenses, but in any actual fight, it would not last long, and Sophia knew it. An old space station reconditioned into a pleasure dome had many weaknesses and, in fact, was quite delicate. "Launch the sparklers and chaff," Sophia commanded.

Zedjack pushed buttons and thousands of small projectiles zipped away from the Merry-Go-Round in all directions. They traveled out away from them and formed an invisible globe. They stopped and hung motionless in space, awaiting a detonation command.

Sophia watched as Manchester and the asteroids recovered from the first barrage. She had jostled them off course and they had to correct their headings. No signs of significant damage. When they had again lined up on the Merry-Go-Round, Sophia knew they would cut loose with a withering response. "Now!" shouted Sophia.

Zedjack pressed the detonator. The invisible globe around the

Merry-Go-Round turned into blinding flashes, fiery explosions and spinning pieces of metal chaff designed to blind the line-of-sight weapons and confuse missile guidance mechanisms. Electronic jamming started at the same time with the same goal, screwing up targeting systems.

Sophia watched as Manchester and the Stoners recovered from the Merry-Go-Round's first volley. He broke radio silence. "OK, boys! Show me what you've got. Our element of surprise is gone. They knew we were coming, so let's get this over with before reinforcements arrive. FIRE!"

What had been an easy target a second ago now looked like a supernova as Sohpia detonated the sparklers and chaff sphere surrounding the Merry-Go-Round. The white light blinded everyone. Line-of-sight shots from laser cannons were guessed. Missiles fired, headed in the right direction, but there was no guarantee they would find the Merry-Go-Round behind a wall of heated, twirling metal. Most of the missiles detonated prematurely, thinking they had reached the hull of the Merry-Go-Round. A few got through and exploded on the defense shields.

The Merry-Go-Round rocked with the effects of the missiles on its defense shields. Everyone on the Midway noticed. It was hard not to feel and hear the thud followed by the rocking motion. No one panicked, but the merrymaking stopped. Everyone headed for their ships and left the Merry-Go-Round. The fringe was notorious for these skirmishes and turf battles, but they did not recommend you hang around while the argument got settled.

Booster Bob and Commander Cody were getting closer all the time, but they still were not there yet. She stopped communicating when the first exchange of fire occurred because she was busy. BB had completed his modification of Sparky and was confident that when the time came, he could agitate the seed pod to pop like the other one had. They had the long-range missile under tow on manual control. Beatrice was far behind with the *Peregrine* lumbering along at top speed. It would be the last to arrive on scene.

"I'm going down to the weapons deck to practice some more with the various systems since we have the time," BB said.

"Good idea. It won't be too long now. I'll call for you when and if we get to that point where we have a clear shot with the seedpod," CC said.

"I'll be ready." BB turned to Duplex, who was flying the ship. "You're doing a great job, Duplex. It really helps to have a pro at the helm."

"I'm not sure I know what that means, but I think it was a compliment?" Duplex said.

BB laughed. "Yes, it was a compliment."

He scurried down to the next deck, where he jumped into the gunner's station. He was getting into this stuff. It was not that long ago that BB had never fired a weapon bigger than a pistol. Now he controlled massive firepower, and he liked the feeling. Plus, he seemed to have a natural knack for it. He started up several practice programs and began running through them.

MGR's first salvo startled Manchester and the Stoners because they didn't expect it. After a couple of Sophia's tricks, now the onslaught had started in earnest. They let loose with laser cannon fire on the Merry-Go-Round, strafing it from one end to the other. Huge impact explosions popped up all over the defense shields, but no damage to the Merry-Go-Round's structure.

A long-range missile showed up on the scene out of nowhere looking for Manchester's *Revenge*. His Defense Officer spotted it coming in and screamed at Manchester to get his attention. It shook him. He wasn't expecting long-range missiles coming into the fight from outside the area locked onto the *Revenge*. Despite the sophisticated anti-missile system detecting it and stopping it, Manchester was distracted.

The *Revenge* rejoined the major attack with its laser cannons, aiming for the command deck. The medium cruiser stationed in front of it deflected much of his fire. Both sides knew that each absorption of a blast diminished their defense shield. It took energy to maintain the defensive bubbles. The Merry-Go-Round was at a disadvantage because of its size.

"Zedjack, get on the *Avenger* and get ready to detach on my command," Sophia said.

He jumped up, turned and ran down the passageway without a word. The Merry-Go-Round was going to be punished.

Sophia knew Manchester and his Stoners were small in comparison to the MGR and that their defense shields would outlast hers. The sparklers and chaff had worked well in deflecting the first attack, but now it would come down to a slugfest between the two. All her weapon stations were operational and had plenty of ammo. Sophia had to time the release of her last surprise, her *Avenger*, just at the point where the Merry-Go-Round's defense shields started to fail. She was playing for time. The longer she lasted, the better chance she had of BB and CC showing up in time to turn the tide of the battle. If she could not last that long, then she would lose the Merry-Go-Round to Manchester. It was that simple.

"Zedjack! Are you ready to go?" she said into her communicator.

"Ready to go on your order," he answered.

"Standby."

The slugfest went on and on with the attackers and the Merry-Go-Round pounding the hell out of each other. Another long-range missile showed up on the scene looking for the *Revenge*. Again, Manchester had to stop and redirect his defenses to destroy it. Sophia was putting up a good fight. Her volume of fire was not as high as theirs, but her accuracy was perfect. Although the defense shields protected Manchester and the Stoners, they still felt each hit inside their crafts. It was like ancient tankers in old wars where metal was the shield that kept projectiles from penetrating. While they survived the hit, the turret shook and rang like a bell. Manchester and the Stoners were being punished the same way. Each hit rattled their crafts, and Sophia did not miss.

Manchester decided now was the time to fire several missiles since he suspected Sophia's defense shields had to be close to complete failure. "Fire two misses, one at the medium cruiser and the other just below it. Let's see if we can't punch a hole in her bubble."

Sophia saw the missiles launched at her on her screen. She checked the defense shield levels. They were down to fifteen percent. This could be the moment.

"Zedjack, wait for the impacts of the two missiles and then, as soon as things stop shaking, disconnect and go after Manchester."

"Happy to oblige."

They waited as the missiles came. The explosions were blinding, and the shield held, but the *Blade* and the Merry-Go-Round trembled like earthquakes had hit them. Alarms went off as the defense shield flickered like a shorted out light bulb. The shaking stopped and Zedjack disconnected the *Avenger* from the Merry-Go-Round.

CHAPTER THIRTY-FOUR

ZEDJACK DISCONNECTED and pulled the *Avenger* away from the Merry-Go-Round's hull. Once clear, he sped up straight for Manchester. The Stoners and Manchester had stopped moving. They pounded the Merry-Go-Round to break down the its defense shield. They were stationary targets from Zedjack's perspective, and for the moment, he had the element of surprise on his side.

"Fire!" Zedjack commanded. They launched a volley of Bruiser missiles. The missiles reached out toward Manchester at blazing speed. These were not the "Devastators" missiles that were four times more powerful. Bruisers were missiles launched in groups to weaken a defense shield. Once locked on, they were impossible to evade. Zedjack had launched three at five-second intervals.

The *Revenge* was too slow in reacting; the "Bruisers" tracked the ship as it sped up and took an almost 90° turn to elude them. The detonations damaged Manchester's defense shield and sent it spinning out of control.

Zedjack swung the *Avenger* around the other side of the Merry-Go-Round with weapons blazing. The Stoners were not moving while they pounded away at the Merry-Go-Round. They stopped firing. To see the *Avenger* come up and over the rim of the Merry-Go-Round blasting away was a surprise as laser cannons hit both of them at the same time. They split in opposite directions as fast as they could go. Defense shields were still intact, but the dynamic character of the engagement had just changed. Now Zedjack's *Avenger* was zipping around, pounding everyone. The overall effect was that the attack on the Merry-Go-Round stopped. This was what Sophia had hoped would happen. It bought her some time to stall until reinforcements arrived. And then the third long-range missile fired by CC and BB at Manchester appeared like magic. The *Revenge* just regained control of its spin in time to destroy it.

BB returned to the command deck and asked, "How are we doing?"

"We are almost there," Duplex said.

"Sophia just contacted us," CC offered as she jumped up to the status board and pointed. "The battle is on. They've been able to hold off Manchester and the Stoners so far. Zedjack with the *Avenger* is causing major problems for them. Manchester believed they had taken out the heavy cruiser and Zedjack, so he's temporarily disoriented, but it won't last. Those three long-range missiles we shot at him a while back worked well."

"I'll bet Manchester was livid with Sophia showing up again where she should not be." BB stared out of the viewport looking ahead. "He will never win this game. She is her own force multiplier. I'm sure he thought he had the advantage of attacking the Merry-Go-Round with Sophia not being onboard to defend it. She outfoxed him again with yet another backup,"

"I want all three of us to look for the right opportunity to unleash our seedpod missile toward Manchester," CC said. "So when things get hot, and they will, let's keep chattering on our communicators so we don't miss the chance to try our secret weapon on him," CC said.

"Why does that sound so desperate?" BB said.

"Because it is, but remember what that thing did to my client's ship when it germinated. It did some serious damage. If we can get it to do that again using your Sparky, then we've got something in store for Manchester that could do some real damage."

"I sure hope it works. OK, I'm going back to my station. It's been an honor and a pleasure serving with you all, you know the rap," BB said. "If we get our butts kicked, hey! We tried. We owe Sophia a shot at ending Manchester's career. Let's do it."

"You almost brought a tear to my eye, but I farted instead," CC said.

"Is that sarcasm or philosophy?" Duplex asked.

BB and CC laughed. Duplex shook her head in confusion and consternation. BB hustled downstairs and strapped himself into his gunner's position. A comm check was done. Everyone settled into a moment of silence. The *Scorpion* was making its last jump. It soon would be there, on the perimeter. They'd better be ready for whatever was going on in the neighborhood.

Manchester's *Revenge* recovered from its spin and headed over the top of the Merry-Go-Round in pursuit of the *Avenger*. It locked onto Zedjack's cruiser and fired a "Slicer," a nuke missile capable of penetrating any defense shield.

"Talk to me, Zedjack. What's happening?" Sophia knew something was going wrong.

"He's launched a nuclear missile at me and it says it can't be defended against," Zedjack screamed. "I don't like this, Sophia."

"Get away from us if you can. I think your shields will hold. Can't believe he's using a nuclear warhead this close to the Merry-Go-Round."

"Aw shit!" Zedjack screamed.

The *Avenger* transformed into an orange-red fireball. The fireball stopped expanding as if tired. Light generated by it dissipated. The shock wave was so strong, it blew the Stoner ship Zedjack was chasing into the Merry-Go-Round, crashing it into a section of the Midway, killing all the Stoners onboard.

"Zedjack? Zedjack?" She refused to believe what she had just witnessed.

Alarms sounded, lights flashed. The Merry-Go-Round stopped the spread of the damage by closing nearby sections with the smoldering remains. Ironic that the Stoner's ship wreckage made it look like an asteroid had hit the Merry-Go-Round.

"Damage report!" Sophia demanded.

System report: "Major damage to Midway section 8. Structure integrity is holding, but unstable. Loss of life: eight crew members, zero clients. Defense Shield is one-hundred-percent down. Gun emplacements are intact and operational. Life support is eighty percent."

"BB and CC." Sophia said over the comms. "Zedjack is gone, along with the *Avenger*. Our defense shields are gone. The Merry-Go-Round has sustained heavy damage. *Blade* is still operational. Hurry. Manchester will be on board soon."

———

Manchester was thrilled. "Finally! One of my investments paid off. That was spectacular... bigger than I was expecting," he said as he picked himself up off the floor. "I have to say Zedjack was tougher and more resilient than I thought, admirable, but in the end, I got him... just like I'm going to get Sophia and her Merry-Go-Round as well. What's our situation?"

"Sir, the explosion blew the Stoner Zedjack was pursuing into the Merry-Go-Round structure. None of the crew of the Stoners survived the explosion. The heavy cruiser is gone, vaporized. It seems the other Stoner is trying to get away, probably back to the asteroid field.

The Merry-Go-Round's defense shields are down. They have a medium cruiser and all gun emplacements are still operational."

"Excellent. How is our defense shield holding up?" Manchester said.

"Sixty percent, sir. Some damage here and there, but fully operational and still fully powered."

"Good. Let's go in for the kill. Does the medium cruiser still have a functional defense shield?"

"Yes, sir, it does."

"Alright, head for the Transportation Dock on the far side. Let's be careful. Sophia is always full of surprises when you least expect them."

CHAPTER THIRTY-FIVE

BOOSTER BOB and Commander Cody viewed the battle surrounding the Merry-Go-Round. They had just finished their last jump. They were in the neighborhood, but didn't want to show up in the middle of the scrap, so they dropped out of their jump at a healthy distance away. Even though they were on separate decks, they both zoomed in on the battle surrounding the Merry-Go-Round when their screens blossomed white. Both of them jumped back.

"That can't be good," BB said over his communicator. "This is not some intergalactic multi-battleship slugfest for the galaxy. It's an alley fight. Who is bringing nukes into this?"

"I agree. It's like bringing a cannon to a knife fight. Has to be Manchester. Let's see if we can replay that to see who just got fried," CC said.

"Not good. This is much worse than I expected. Manchester is going to rush her now, since she just lost Zedjack's *Avenger* and her defense shields. We have to hurry." CC got up and joined Duplex at the controls.

BB had already lost Sophia once to the parallel world, and he did not want to lose her again. His emotions had no effect on what was going on right now. The Merry-Go-Round was getting pounded by

Manchester and his asteroid friend. They were on the outskirts of the skirmish, but not there yet. "Let's try to target Manchester with our seed pod missile," BB said.

"Do you want to lock on to him or try to steer it yourself all the way in?" CC asked.

"Yes. Let's launch it from here and I'll steer it into him. He expects us, but he doesn't expect a long-range missile coming in from left field way ahead of us. Let's do it."

"OK, I just released control of it. You've got it from there. Is Sparky connected and running?"

"Affirmative. I'm speeding it up to full speed now. Hope it all works," BB said.

"So do it," CC said.

The missile with the seed pod attached to the nose of it lit up and took off, headed toward the fight. BB focused on his guidance monitor, getting the feel of his controls. Sparky was on and humming. He felt like some ancient warrior bringing a crossbow to a laser cannon fight. *Stop thinking like that,* he told himself. It was worth a try.

———

Manchester fired on several gun emplacements, destroying them. With the Merry-Go-Round's defense shield down, he neutralized all of them on the side he was facing. Then he turned off his defense shield and headed toward the Merry-Go-Round's transportation deck to board it. The last Stoner and Sophia's *Blade* would fight on the opposite side of the Merry-Go-Round. It was an even match with no winner apparent yet. Manchester wanted to get onto Merry-Go-Round and take it over before Sophia's reinforcements arrived.

"Sir, we have a single missile headed our way. Strange, though, it does not have a warhead signature," the defense officer said.

"Then what's the point?" Manchester said. "Let's see a long-range visual of it." It was a small and fast weapon with something attached to the nose. "What the hell is that?" No answers came from anyone in his crew. "Laser cannons! Take it out. We'll land with our assault team and take over the Merry-Go-Round. We'll send the *Revenge* to stop Sophia and her reinforcements. Move!"

Sophia 3 was in a critical situation. Her defense shield was dead. The Stoner that was blown into the Merry-Go-Round when Manchester took out Zedjack destroyed a section of the Midway. They successfully isolated and sealed off the section with drones and androids. She had lost her gun emplacements on one side of the MGR when the defense shield died. Manchester headed to the transportation deck to land an assault team. BB and CC were coming fast, but not fast enough.

BB somehow could anticipate the laser cannon volley each time they fired at the seedpod missile. Just before they would fire, he would jerk the joystick and make the missile jump up, down, or sideways, making them miss. Manchester's ship stopped shooting as it dropped off the assault team. Then it pulled back out, turned toward the incoming missile, and resumed firing. BB pulled a gamer move sideways and sped up. He grabbed his Sparky and activated the program. The seedpod did not respond.

"Shit!" BB yelled. "Come on. I know this annoys you." He realized he was cursing at a seedpod strapped to a missile heading into a battle. "Am I crazy? Of course I'm crazy. Show me the magic now. Come on, you can do it."

The seedpod turned warm, then it glowed.

"YES!" BB had to time it just right while still jumping around to avoid being hit by the laser cannons. If he did not do it right, it would be like throwing a rock at a metal ball. It would just bounce off harmlessly. He focused like a laser beam.

Manchester and his team raced across the transportation flight deck as he watched his *Revenge* take off and fight the incoming missile. Laser cannons started blazing away when a streak came in from the right and penetrated. Seconds passed. His ship jerked into a violent roll as an internal explosion blew parts of the *Revenge* out and away from it. He stopped in his tracks, staring at his ship as it disintegrated in slow-motion. That was not a normal detonation. Green tendrils came out of the gaping holes on both sides of his ship. They made his ship look like a hybrid monster of metal and organic tentacles. He had seen something like this before, back at the skirmish with Sophia, Booster Bob, and Commander Cody beyond the Black Wall. There was a thing there too that was growing in the vastness of nothing. Was that the secret cargo that Commander Cody had delivered out there? Had another devil seed germinated inside his ship? Several escape pods shot out of Manchester's ship toward the Merry-Go-Round's transportation deck.

"Woot! Woot!" screamed CC. "The seed has germinated successfully inside of Manchester's ship. It disabled the *Revenge*. Manchester has boarded the Merry-Go-Round with an assault team. I'm sure you know this already, Sophia. BB and I are coming in hot to join the *Blade*, who is engaged with the Stoner ship on your far side."

"Got it, CC. Hell of a shot with the seedpod, BB. Congrats! You are good. We'll hold off Manchester and his group as long as we can. Be warned I'm activating another backup of myself. We need all the bodies and weapons we can find onboard. Good luck in taking out the Stoner," Sophia said.

Duplex brought the *Scorpion* into a 90° vector on the Stoner. BB opened fire with everything he had. The sheer volume of fire knocked the Stoner sideways. His defense shield was still working, but going bad fast. BB started thinking about what he had heard Sophia say during the last transmission. She was going to activate her backup for extra help in fighting off Manchester. Two Sophias! Could BB handle a threesome? How could he be thinking about this in the middle of a battle? Easy; it turned him on.

The *Scorpion* and *Blade* advanced on the Stoner, unleashing withering fire. The strikes buffeted the Stoner. The noise and shockwaves inside the Stoner's ship were reaching a critical mass. Crew members were holding their hands to their ears to stop the noise. Their commander made a run for it.

With a damaged and diminishing defense shield, running was a better option. In fact, it was the only option they had. The Stoner sped up low across the surface of the Merry-Go-Round, using it as insurance against being shot at as he made his getaway. Both medium cruisers pursued him. As he came up and over the arch of the Merry-Go-Round he spotted Manchester's craft being devoured by a wild weed monster. As he pulled away from the scene, alarms went off. He headed directly toward the *Peregrine* as it arrived on the scene. Before the Stoner could even react, the *Peregrine* opened fire on it.

"OK, boys! Unless you have a strong death wish, the game is over. How about you turn off your engines, your weapons, and surrender right now?" CC made it sound more like a demand than an ask. The Stoner's crew looked at each other and agreed they were done. They shut everything down and waited for further instructions from CC.

CHAPTER THIRTY-SIX

THE BATTLE outside the Merry-Go-Round was over. BB and CC boarded the Stoner ship, made sure everything was turned off and put the crew of three onto a shuttle headed for the *Peregrine* to be locked up.

"We have to move fast and get on board the Merry-Go-Round before Manchester and his crew take over the place," BB said.

"Agreed. He took out most of the gun emplacements before he boarded the Merry-Go-Round. Duplex, head for the transportation bay. Crew, suit up for combat and standby."

She felt odd giving Sophia's crew orders, but they didn't seem to mind under the circumstances. They sped up toward the transport deck on the underside. "Contact the *Blade* and tell them to join us in the transport deck for the party. Beatrice, once we're onboard, pull the *Peregrine* in closer to the Merry-Go-Round and train all your weapons on her. If our skirmish with Manchester goes bad, I want you to blow it to pieces, Manchester with it," CC said.

"Aye! Aye! Commander," Beatrice said.

CC chuckled to herself. Beatrice knew CC loved that kind of shit talk. She would salute her and shout orders like it was a Battle Starship, and the funny thing was it always made her feel better. Sick.

As the *Scorpion* slowed to enter the transport bay, BB marveled at the scene going on in and around Manchester's splendid super fighter, the *Revenge*. It looked like they had shot it with a gigantic shotgun. There were holes all over the hull and some of those holes had green tentacles coming out of them that wrapped around the outside of the ship. "He can't be happy about that," BB said.

Manchester stared at his *Revenge*, frozen. His escaping crew members landed on the Merry-Go-Round's transport deck in their escape pods and scrambled out of them to report to him. "What the hell happened?" Manchester screamed.

"Sir, we don't know for sure. As it came in at us, it expected our every shot. Just as we'd pull the trigger, it would jump sideways, and we'd miss. The thing on the nose of it glowed red and purple, sort of pulsating. It sliced through our defense shield like it wasn't there and penetrated the hull. Then it exploded or germinated and ate two of our crew, so we jumped into the escape pods and landed here," he said.

"What is it? It looks organic, not mechanical?"

"Sir, you've got me. I have seen nothing like this in my lifetime and I've been all over this galaxy."

"Can't do much about it now, damn it. Let's move. Sophia is waiting for us, and I don't want to disappoint her. I will not let that wire head beat me again. I'm taking over this place now. Move out." Manchester had twelve heavily armed crew members with him. He had a new device that, if it worked, should take care of his nemesis Sophia. "The command center is next floor up. Her crew lacks fighting experience. Most of them are security types. They know how to use their weapons, but know nothing about tactics. Don't underestimate them, but they should not be a problem." They moved toward elevators and ladders, keeping in touch and coordinated via their communicators.

Sophia listened in on Manchester's chatter with his assault group and those escaping from the doomed *Revenge*. She directed her forces to various areas to intercept them. She hoped to pick off a few and delay Manchester's advance so BB and CC could show up with reinforcements. That was the plan. An enormous hole in that plan was that she expected Zedjack to be there with his crew, but he and his crew were dead. Things did not look good right now. Manchester was right, most of her security crew were not fighters. They did not lack loyalty or courage, but they lacked combat experience.

Sophia 3 played her last card by activating her backup. She needed as much help as she could find, so all hands were on deck. "Sophia 4, happy to meet you... I mean, me. Not sure how this is going to work out, but for now, you are in charge. If you get zapped, then I'll be in charge. Does that sound good?"

"Sounds great to me," Sophia 4 said. "Let's set up on opposite sides of the opening gate to the Midway. He's expecting one of us, but not two. If two, then maybe he'll think there is even more. At least it'll be another surprise that we can capitalize on, I hope."

Manchester's point man held up his hand to hold. Sophia's security crew had blocked the main access passageway to the command deck with a jerry-rigged gun setup. This would not take long to overcome, but it would take time. His crew fanned out and split into two groups on either side of the wide passageway. Manchester's force moved forward, Sophia released smoke into the tunnel. Visibility dropped to zero. Both sides started firing blindly, hoping to do damage. The gun Sophia's crew was using was an antique. A .30 caliber belt-fed machine gun. They pulled it out of a historical display, but it worked. It was loud, and it threw out a blanket of bullets that filled the smoke filled tunnel. The ricochets filled the corridor with zinging hot metal. The

Merry-Go-Round crew killed one of Manchester's group and wounded another.

The fire from Manchester's gang was effective as well. Laser streams ripped into the makeshift wall with full effect. A cannon shot hit the barricade and took out the machine gun, along with its operators. The rest of the security crew scampered away down the hallway under the cover of smoke.

He knew he had hit the barricade, but could not tell if there were still defenders there waiting to pick them off. Manchester commanded, "Stay put for a second until we see what we are dealing with. How many were wounded?"

"One dead and another wounded, sir."

"Shit! Hold tight."

Sophia had infrared detectors showing her they had stopped moving because of the smoke, so she added more smoke.

It did not take Manchester long to figure out that more smoke was being piped in, so he ordered them to move out. When they reached the barricade, they could see the damage they had done, but the defenders had retreated. "Move out fast. She is trying to stall until her buddies show up."

BB and CC ran down the exit ramp of the *Scorpion*, along with Duplex and the rest of the crew. Everyone had weapons and suits ready for combat. Manchester's escape pods littered the transport deck. The *Blade* slowly glided in and landed next to them. Both crews ran up the corridor into the first air lock with BB, CC and Duplex leading the way. They ran into the smoke screen lingering in the passageway when they exited the airlock. There was no visibility, so they held in place and sent two ahead to scout out the situation. Manchester could be waiting for them.

BB tried to contact Sophia, "Sophia, are you there? What's your status?" Silence. "Sophia, what's going on? We are here working our way up the entrance corridor. Lots of smoke, so we're taking it slow."

"They are almost to the command deck. We are pulling back out into the Midway entrance dome to set up defensive positions. Hurry!" Sophia said.

That was it. They were on the move. No more communications. BB stood and said, "Corridor is clear. Move out." They caught up with their scouts at the destroyed barricade and continued moving toward the command deck.

Manchester and his team arrived at the command deck, meeting no resistance. The Merry-Go-Round was functioning. It displayed various systems on screens around the deck. Sophia must have just left. Seats were still warm. He would destroy the Merry-Go-Round if that was what it took to eliminate Sophia. If he could kill her and take control of the Merry-Go-Round still in one piece, well, that was the grand prize he had been after all along. "Nothing here. Move out to the entrance to the Midway." They hustled down the corridor that led to the Midway.

The entrance of the Merry-Go-Round had a transparent dome that showed the stars and the other side of the circular structure. Two balconies surrounded the dome, allowing more vantage points. Sophia and her crew had built a barrier across the Midway entrance and at strategic locations on the balconies. She had instructed her crew to open fire on Manchester's crew as soon as they tried to enter the dome area to keep them bottled up in the corridor.

Sophia 4 was at the other end of the first balcony, as Sophia 3 had requested. They waited. Sophia's infrared detectors showed them close to the dome's entrance. Two of Manchester's crew entered the area. The barrier and both opposing balconies opened fire. They killed one and wounded another. He crawled to safety behind a column. Manchester now knew where her defensive positions were located. The fire fight that followed was brutal. Both sides took casualties. The Sophias had not shown themselves yet. Manchester's forces had worked their way into the main dome area using columns and structure outcroppings as cover. It was time for Sophia to confront Manchester once and for all.

CHAPTER THIRTY-SEVEN

SOPHIA 3 WAS up on the second balcony. The cable from the apex of the dome came down and she draped it over the balcony railing next to her. She grabbed it, hopped up onto the railing and jumped off, swinging out across the battlefield below. As she zoomed across holding onto the cable with one hand, she sprayed Manchester's position with laser fire from her other arm. The effect was stunning. Three of Manchester's soldiers were dead on her first pass. They all looked up and started firing at her. She had micro propulsion blasters located all over her body, just below the skin. Sophia 3 made short blasts, one here, one there, just enough to make them miss her from below. It was subtle and effective.

As Manchester stood up, he pulled something out of his jacket and aimed it at Sophia 3 as she flew in all directions. It did not look like much, like a chromed pointer. He activated it and a green beam of light filled with energy streamed toward Sophia 3. It grew wider as it got closer to her, so she could not maneuver out of the way. When it hit her, she fell forty feet like a stone to the floor and bounced like a rag doll. Parts of her broke off from the impact. Both sides froze, staring at her lying lifeless on the floor.

BB, CC and Duplex could hear the firefight echoing down the corridor as they drew closer. Then the fighting sound stopped all at once.

"Sophia! What's happening? We're almost there. Hold on!" BB screamed into his communicator as he ran.

"Manchester has some kind of weapon that kills robots in a single shot. He shot Sophia 3 down in an instant. She activated me as a precaution, but now I'm not sure how to fight his weapon," Sophia 4 said. "I am afraid, but I will try."

She sounded bewildered, which was so out of character for her. Then again, seeing yourself snuffed out like that in front of you would have that effect.

"Sophia! Please don't put yourself in danger. We're almost there," BB said.

Manchester's gang had set up a rapid-fire laser gun in the rear to stop BB, CC and the crew coming up the corridor. They let loose on the group as they came out of the tunnel into the dome area. Sophia 4 saw what was happening and sprang into action. She revealed herself on the second balcony on the opposite side where Sophia 3 had swung down from and started firing on Manchester's frontline. The pitch of the battle resumed.

Manchester shook his head. "How many Sophias do I have to kill to take over this damn place? She's multiplying on me." He pulled out his shiny device again and tried to aim it at Sophia, but her firing was intense and accurate, so it was hard to get a shot off.

BB and CC rolled into the room with their weapons firing. The volume of fire from Manchester's gun setup pinned them down. Duplex ran into the room and dove headfirst across the floor, sliding on her belly. She was already in a better position than any of their forces. Manchester's gun setup was causing casualties at the entrance.

BB saw Sophia up on the balcony blazing away at Manchester below. She was still alive... he was so happy to see her. As his eyes swept the room, he saw another destroyed Sophia lying dead in pieces in the middle of the floor. "What is going on here?" BB pointed toward the body while looking at CC close to him, behind a pillar. The noise of the battle was too loud to hear each other say anything. CC looked in the direction he pointed at and shook her head. BB knew Sophia had backups of herself, but rarely did she ever have more than one activated at a time. She used to say it was too much competition.

Both sides were lobbing grenades and firing bigger shells at each other. Damage was mounting, along with casualties on both sides. Sophia's position was becoming untenable. She moved by jumping. Over the railing, she went down two stories until her blasters broke her fall and she landed as light as a ballerina.

Manchester rose and fired at the spot where she was landing. The eerie green beam shot across the room and caught Sophia just as she touched the floor. The light went out of her eyes. She crumpled over into a heap on the floor. Gone.

BB's heart froze. CC's head dropped forward onto her chest. After all they had been through to have it end this way in the home stretch was more than devastating, but there it was... Sophia was no longer with them, none of them. The battle stopped as soon as Sophia 4 fell. BB wanted to go out avenging Sophia's death, but who was he kidding? He was not a warrior. His spark box was worthless here. He had lost her forever.

Manchester stood and commanded his troops to cease fire. CC did the same. What was the point now?

"I declare the Merry-Go-Round mine, since the owner is now dead," Manchester announced.

"Not so fast, asshole," someone said.

Manchester turned around slowly to see who had said it.

Duplex stood forty feet away.

Manchester recognized her, and yet she looked different somehow. "Who in the hell are you?"

"I am your nemesis. I am also the next in line in the dynasty."

"Dynasty? What dynasty?"

"The Merry-Go-Round dynasty," Duplex said.

Manchester burst into laughter. "Like royalty, eh? So let me understand you. Somehow, some way, you see yourself stepping into Sophia's role because of what? Make believe? Your fantasy maybe? Listen, you goddamned wire head, I'm taking over the Merry-Go-Round and that's all there is to it."

He pulled out his chrome device, aimed it at her, and fired. The green beam engulfed Duplex. Nothing happened. It had no effect. Manchester fired again. Duplex smiled. He fired again and again. He might as well have been shining a cheap flashlight. Manchester was furious.

"Who are you? Why didn't it work on you?" he screamed.

"I am Sophia, from another world. Your magic does not work on me here."

Her right arm came up so fast, it was hard to see. There was a flash from her arm with a loud crack!

Manchester looked surprised at how fast it all happened. He threw his shiny new device away in disgust. Staggering a step, he turned around to face his crew. Their expressions told him everything he needed to know. Looking down at the front of his body, he saw pieces of fabric from his suit smoldering. Blood ran down the front of him from his mouth. Staggering, he dropped to his knees and felt his midsection with his hands. There was a hole in the middle of him about the size of a bowling ball. Gasping, he swung his head up toward the top of the dome and screamed, "It's not fair...!!!" and fell face first onto the deck. A pool of blood grew under him in slow motion as he bled out. His crew dropped their weapons and raised their hands. It was over again.

Silence invaded the scene of carnage. No one moved for many seconds. Drifting clouds of smoke high above looked like clouds inside the dome.

Booster Bob and Commander Cody looked at each other.

"I'm so glad Duplex is here," CC said.

BB nodded his head in agreement. "I don't know how she did that, but she did. Manchester always underestimated what robots could do. In the end, it proved to be his demise. Sophia knew that."

Everyone started moving at once. They apprehended the survivors of Manchester's crew. Medical support arrived to help those wounded and others began the cleanup.

The less damaged Sophia was in a sitting position on the floor, slumped as if she was resting, and BB walked over to her. He sat down next to her. Remarkably, there was not a mark on her, no sign of injury, but now she was just a piece of metal and synthetic flesh. BB held her to him and rocked back and forth, gently talking to her in whispers. A horrible noise startled him. It was him, sobbing. It shook him to his core; his tears fell like rain. He lost track of time telling her all the things he should have told her before like how much he loved her. After a long while, BB got up to his feet holding Sophia. He found a couple of gurneys and carefully loaded both Sophias onto them. Duplex and CC came forward to help him move them out of the dome area. They slowly wheeled them away.

Duplex took control of the Merry-Go-Round like she thought Sophia would want. She knew nothing about the place. How could she? She was from another universe. Yes, it was like the Bird's Nest enterprise in her world, but this was very different. That was not her concern now. She had another priority.

CHAPTER THIRTY-EIGHT

BB, along with a sobbing CC and Duplex, wheeled the gurneys down the corridor leading away from the battle area. "I have no idea where I'm going," BB realized.

Both CC and Duplex had no idea either. "Excuse me," BB said as he stopped someone in the hallway. "Can you tell me where the engineering or maintenance area is located?"

"Two floors down, Section E, you can't miss it," the person said.

"Thanks." BB looked at Duplex and said, "So I have to ask you why didn't Manchester's robot destroyer work on you? You said something about his magic didn't work on you. How is that?"

"Sophia's operating system has memory banks, artificial intelligence, and multiplexing systems that work together. Manchester's shiny toy is a quantum eraser coupled with a powerful projector. If you run on an operating system and you get hit with his ray gun, it wipes out everything in an instant. You are wiped clean and cease to function. It doesn't physically touch anything."

"But you have an operating system or I would not have been able to jack into you and stimulate you."

"Yes. I function just like Sophia, but the difference is we developed a shell that shields all my internal systems from that kind of weapon. It was a necessity during our war in order to defend ourselves."

"Too bad she could not communicate that information to the Sophias on this side in time to build them and wear them for protection," he said. "Guess she told you about our couple of adventures, right?"

"Yes, she told me. Booster Bob made her very happy, and she felt she had done the same for you," Duplex said.

"Ha! You could say that she matched me, which is extraordinary, considering my level of experience versus her first try. I think I'll leave it at that."

Duplex smiled this time. "BB, I know losing Sophia is devastating for you, but I want to ask you a hypothetical question."

"Sure. What is it?"

"Remember the shiny oval thing that looked like a silver river stone I gave you?"

"Yes, I remember."

"Do you still have it?"

"I'm sure I do." BB started going through all the pockets of his flight suit. He pulled out the small metallic round object. It was still intact. They both stopped walking and stared at it together. BB let out a funny short sound, not a yell, or gasp, but a mixture of Eureka! And Holy shit! "I get it. This is Sophia. I'm holding her in my hand if I can figure out a way to reinstall her and reboot her!"

"What do you think?" Duplex asked.

"Monster challenge here. If she had an operating system, running it would take two seconds to download this into her and BINGO! She'd be back, but she is dead. Nothing to grab hold of inside to get her going again. There has to be a way. Let me think," BB said.

They started walking again toward the Engineering Section. BB's mood was improving. He loved solving problems, and it motivated him. Could they revive Sophia? They lifted the undamaged version of Sophia onto a large workbench in the center of the bay. They grounded her. He pulled out Sparky and jacked it into the back of

Sophia's head and turned it on. Nobody home. No trace of anything left. It depressed him. She had been such an effervescent entity and had developed a multi-faceted personality that was thought impossible in a robot. One of a kind... and he loved her.

Duplex watched as BB sketched out diagrams, rifled through algorithms, and scanned his equipment. She could tell he was getting frustrated. "Any luck?" she said.

"Not really. No matter how I approach it, I always end up coming back to the same place. Without an active operating system to tap into, I have no options. If I had that, then anything is possible."

"I have an idea. What if I could inject myself into Sophia through Sparky? If we could jump start her processor and get it to latch onto my operating system, then you could install Sophia over the top of me as an upgrade. Wouldn't that work, maybe?"

"Duplex, it would erase you in an instant. Sophia's essence would obliterate all of you. There would be no way of retrieving you. Do you understand that?" BB said.

"I understand. Look BB, you were not there, but when the battle in my world was coming to that moment when we had to do something drastic, Sophia did not hesitate to make that decision. She sacrificed herself so that we would prevail. I owe her big time. While I will no longer exist, I will become a part of her, and that's not an unpleasant thought."

BB stared into Duplex's eyes. "You've already done so much for us. You killed Manchester just as he was about to take over the Merry-Go-Round. That should be enough," BB said.

"Sophia would not agree with you. I do not agree with you. It's all about love and loyalty in the end. I insist."

"I do not know if this scheme will even work. What if I cannot bring Sophia back and destroy you as well in the attempt?"

"At least you tried. That's what counts," Duplex said.

"I will research, investigate and tinker with this idea and see if I can build some kind of approach to this. If I think I've got something that will work, then we'll see. I can't commit yet, Duplex. You understand."

Duplex nodded her head in agreement. She gave him a memory pod. "These are all the details of my specifications. They should be helpful." Then she walked out of the Engineering Section.

BB sat down next to the inert Sophia and whispered to her, "Don't get your hopes up, but maybe..." He started working on new arrangements and diagrams with a vengeance.

Duplex joined CC in the dome. Cleanup had started. The place was a mess. Holes in the walls, burn marks, and blood stains stood as witnesses to the rumble. The Merry-Go-Round crew moved the wounded to the sick bay. The dead were being collected as well.

"I'll bet if Sophia was with us, she'd make an exhibition of all this somehow..." CC said.

"She was a genius at finding nirvana in a pile of trash. I'm sure you're right," Duplex said.

"You know, we all need to sit down and discuss all of this. I didn't have any problem taking command way out there on the other side of the Black Wall, but I'm not so sure I want the job now that the fight is over," CC said.

"I'm not an excellent candidate either," Duplex said. "BB would not want the job either, I don't think. It's Sophia's creation. She needs to run it since she fought hard for it and deserves it."

"That's for sure, but now that's not possible," CC sighed.

"BB is working on that. Don't rule out her resurrection too soon. Booster Bob is tinkering."

"Whoa! Wouldn't that be a sweet ending?" CC said.

Booster Bob had to stop to get something to eat and take a brief nap or he would pass out from exhaustion. He had been experimenting with several ideas that might work. Now he had to make the physical modifications to Sparky and start testing to see if he was right. The whole time, he would glance over at Sophia lying on the bench top, so dark and still, and redouble his efforts, hoping to bring her back.

In the kitchen, he ate something that came out of a machine and drank water. He lay down for a quick nap on a long lounge seat. His dreams were vivid. Sophia sat up and said to him, "What's taking so long, BB? I'm tired of waiting. We have so much to do together. Show me your magic. I believe in you."

"I can do it... I know I can!" BB woke himself up, screaming out loud. He had been out for half an hour, but it was all he needed. After grabbing a big cup of coffee, he headed back to the Engineering Section and resumed his work.

The only scenario BB could come up with was transferring Duplex, all of her systems, into Sophia while jump starting Sophia's power supply. BB programmed Duplex's operating system to look for and find the power source. Once it found it and locked on to it, it would initialize Duplex's operating system and distribute all the other parts of her to their proper locations. If that was accomplished, the rest was easy. BB could import Sophia into herself from the backup, which would overwrite Duplex entirely. Sophia would wake up and Duplex would evaporate. Regain Sophia at the cost of Duplex. It was a hard reality and yet it was the only alternative if he wanted to bring Sophia back. He had to keep reminding himself that Sophia had sacrificed herself in a parallel world to save Duplex and her group. Duplex was eager to return the favor. Brutal decision to make. Booster Bob was now convinced that there was no other option. He made his modifications. BB ran tests on all of them and they proved viable. Building the setup took time. He did not want any mistakes. It was now ready. One last glance at Sophia before he walked out of the Engineering Section up toward the Command Deck. He whispered to her again, "Hope this works. I miss you so much."

CHAPTER THIRTY-NINE

As BB entered the command deck area, he saw CC and Duplex sitting by the Merry-Go-Round's main console, talking. He walked up to them. They both stopped talking and looked up at him. "I'm ready if you are... Duplex, I want to ask you one more time if you are sure you want to do this?"

She smiled and said, "I am not thrilled about ending my existence, but I am sure about what I'm doing for Sophia. I owe her. It's time to repay my debt. I tried to tell Sophia I can't be duplicated or backed up like she could be. It has to do with a self-replicating block built into my operating system. So I'm one of a kind. I have enjoyed my new freedom and fighting alongside both of you."

"Not an optimal time for you to cross over into a new parallel world," CC said. "It seems both worlds, at least our minor part of them, were in the middle of a turf battle. It's been an honor to fight alongside you as well. Without your help, we would not have succeeded."

"That means a lot to me coming from you, Commander Cody. Goodbye." Duplex stood up and joined BB as they walked back toward the Engineering Section.

"Everything CC just said goes for me too. Not only did you take out Manchester at the last moment, but you are sacrificing yourself so we can get our beloved Sophia back," BB said.

"It will thrill her to see you, Booster Bob. She talked about you all the time when we weren't busy fighting off the bad guys. The best part of what I am doing is bringing you two back together again. I am at peace with myself. My memories will go with me when I die, just like you humans."

Duplex's simple assessment and expression of emotion surprised BB. They arrived in the Engineering Section. Sophia looked so lonely lying there, still on the slab. BB helped Duplex onto a long table he had set up next to Sophia. She lay back and put her arms down by her sides. She turned her head and looked at BB.

"It has been a great experience knowing you, Booster Bob. Do your thing and say hello to Sophia for me. I'll put myself on standby now." And she did.

BB stood looking down on Duplex and Sophia. He believed in himself, but he was human, and humans made mistakes. His mind raced through all the details of the setup and the programming, trying to see if there was anything he had overlooked. Nothing that he could think of, so he reached for his Sparky, which now looked like a game controller on steroids with all the wires and cables coming out of it. It was showtime. He flipped the power switch on and jacked Duplex into it. Duplex and Sophia were both connected to Sparky. The display showed everything was ready to go. He hit the GO key. BB flashed back to his first session with Sophia and how that had turned into a disaster that was not his fault. He was determined to make this conversion a success.

"OK, well, that's a good sign," BB said to himself. "Sophia has got power, but nothing else. Need to introduce Duplex into her framework and see if the power supply latches onto Duplex's operating system." More tapping on his spark box. He focused so hard, it hurt. Nothing happened. He waited, still nothing. "Shit! Didn't work. Only one more thing to try, different logarithm, turn on AI nanobots." He had written two different strategies. This first one bombed; no dice.

His second approach was all he had left and it was even more radical. Even with all the specs that Duplex had given him about herself, she was still a different breed of robot. BB could not master all those differences fast enough, but maybe AI driven nanobots could with a little luck.

BB was deep down into his own process. It would be an extraordinary feat if he was successful this time. BB's second run was immediate. His last attempt was running through Duplex into Sophia. He waited. Nothing. Still nothing, BB jumped when Sparky told him it was "Working." "OK, now be nice. Introduce yourselves to each other. Find common ground, make connections if possible, persuade and, please oh please, agree to reboot and unite as one...." he pleaded. "This could take a while," he said to himself.

Sophia's body twitched. That was a wonderful sign, BB thought. They were trying to work it out. *Let them do it, give them all the time they need.* He backed away for a second. Both robots were trembling. Then Duplex went slack and still. Sophia's eyes fluttered and opened.

"Duplex, you made it. You are in Sophia's body now. How does it feel?" BB said.

Silence lingered. Sophia's eyes opened and shut several times. "You were right. Sophia's body differs from mine in many small ways. I am delighted to be here once again, if only for a little while. Congratulations, Booster Bob. You have been successful," Duplex's voice said through Sophia.

"How do you feel, Duplex? Is there anything that you are missing in terms of internal functioning?" BB asked.

"I feel eerie. I think that is the right word. Everything is functioning, but there are hundreds of differences that I notice and my system wants to accommodate and change them. I resist that urge, since there is no point in doing so since I am a temporary inhabitant of Sophia's body."

BB was still adjusting to having Duplex's voice come out of Sophia's mouth. That was eerie too. "Try to relax if you can and let me run some system checks to verify that one hundred percent of you arrived inside of Sophia's body."

"OK. Are you excited?" Duplex said.

"Excited?"

"Yes, excited. You are one step closer to being reunited with your beloved Sophia," Duplex said. Sophia's head turned sideways and gazed at Duplex's empty body lying next to her. "Seems odd to be outside of my body."

"Of course I'm excited. Yes, I imagine it is weird to see yourself lying next to you. I am going to run my system checks now." BB tapped keys and pushed buttons while watching the readouts. The AI nanobots had worked it all out on their own. Sophia's systems accepted Duplex's unique programs. No damage was done and Duplex had let no modifications occur to Sophia's infrastructure. That was very important when it came time to replace Duplex with Sophia's backup. They had talked about how important it was before they started the transfer.

"All of you made the transfer over the bridge into Sophia. Now we'll update you with Sophia's full backup." BB inserted the chrome memory pod into a rigged-up reader that was connected to his spark box. "I guess it is time to say goodbye and to thank you again for what you have done for us and for what you are about to do for us."

"It has been a privilege to join you all in the fight. I'm glad I could help. I owe Sophia so much that doing this is the least I can do. Please say goodbye to CC for me."

"Goodbye, Duplex!" CC shouted.

BB jumped and turned to see CC coming up behind them.

"Love you, kid. Thanks for saving our asses." Tears ran down CC's cheeks.

Duplex in Sophia's body raised up enough to see CC and wave to her. Then she lay back down.

"How long have you been here?" BB asked CC.

"Long enough to see your Dr. Frankenstein skills in action." She smiled through her tears.

"My what?"

"Never mind. Get back to what you were doing." CC pointed at Duplex.

"Let's do this thing, Booster Bob." Duplex closed her eyes.

BB pressed the Enter key on Sparky, and everything went into slow motion. It was as if Duplex's operating system did not want to give up its existence that easily, so there was some resistance here and there. He expected this and had written some code to accommodate it. This process would take some time. It would either work or it would not...

CHAPTER FORTY

BB WALKED BACK to where CC was sitting. "You know this is tearing me apart too. Duplex saved our butts."

"You got that right." She shrugged. "It's so hard to lose close friends when you've been through so much together."

"I want both Sophia and Duplex to be here. I wish there was another way, but I couldn't find it. The hardest part is over, I think. This part will take some time. Replacing Duplex with Sophia is easy, but it is tedious because so many things have to be redone and optimized. It should work because I have eliminated compatibility issues, but nothing is for certain."

"Whatever, I get the concept, but not the details. So if you save Sophia, then what are you going to do?"

"Good question. To be honest, I do not know. I have not thought that far ahead yet. If I can pull this off, I will feel like I've come full circle. What started as a special session with the owner of the Merry-Go-Round turned into an adventure that ended up back where it started."

A beeping sound started. "She's getting ready to do a full restart sequence, the moment of truth." he said as he turned away from CC and returned to Sophia's side. He scanned his Sparky and other monitors. No red lights anywhere. He punched the "Continue" button... the process started. Three hours passed. Lights and sounds created a staccato symphony. Then all went silent. BB drew closer to Sophia.

Nothing but stillness. He waited as so many emotions flew through his head and heart. Was that a sound he heard? Could it be? Her eyes opened bright and wide. She rolled her head to the side, which wasn't easy with the cables still attached, and focused on BB's face. "I told you it wasn't your fault."

"So you did," BB said, with tears running down his face now. He disconnected her from Sparky and hugged her.

CC ran up crying and joined the hug. As they unwrapped from each other, BB stopped and stared at Duplex's carcass, lying still next to them. "Thank you, Duplex. You saved us all today. We will love and remember you forever."

With all of Sophia's precautions and backups, she still lost part of her experiences and memories. Duplex gave BB a backup of Sophia's life, which included her sacrifice in a parallel world to save Duplex's people. She knew nothing of the last battle with Manchester, including her demise and Manchester's. It took time to update her on everything, including the Merry-Go-Round's damage caused by a nearby nuclear missile blast. Sophia was grateful to hear how Manchester met his end at the hands of Duplex. That gave her real satisfaction. She felt she helped to bring her to this side and Duplex ended up saving them all.

CC helped with the aftermath as much as she could. To fix the Merry-Go-Round, Sophia ordered many construction materials from nearby sources. CC transported them all. BB and Sophia had disappeared for days to Sophia's living quarters, with strict instructions not to be disturbed. They were together all the time as the Merry-Go-Round recovered. CC was happy for them. Several times, she thought it was time to leave and go back to running freight around the galaxy, but Sophia kept finding more for her to do. They talked her into putting her bowling ball on exhibit so that customers could see themselves in a parallel world. Sophia let her keep all the proceeds from that, so CC became rich in a brief time. To fulfill her desire for space travel, they transformed *Peregrine* into a fancy bus to take people to and from the Merry-Go-Round.

BB and Sophia turned the Merry-Go-Round into an improved destination spot. It had been popular before as a last-minute stop for travelers as they left or entered the galaxy. It became the place to go to, stay awhile, have fun and see the actual results of a turf war. They turned the crashed Stoners' asteroid ship into an exhibit. They preserved the punctured hole through which the Stoners' ship had crashed. It fascinated visitors.

Manchester's *Revenge* was popular too. The bizarre organic plant that now inhabited it was a popular draw, especially around feeding time, like in a zoo. Its tentacles would start swinging around as it caught organic food that Sophia's crew would toss into it. It turned out to be a perfect symbiotic relationship. Folks found it entertaining to watch it feed as the whole thing rotated in slow motion a few hundred yards out from the Merry-Go-Round.

The debris field left by the *Avenger* was enormous. They used it as a shooting gallery for customers. They loved shooting away at pieces large and small with a different array of weapons. At first, Sophia had been concerned about the bodies of Zedjack and his crew, but after extensive searching, they could find nothing left of them. The nuke had vaporized everything organic. Sophia initially thought Zedjack would like the shooting gallery, but then decided against it. The ghosts of Zedjack and his crew haunted her. She closed it down because she and BB felt it was disrespectful and too sad for them to continue. They moved the shooting gallery to the other side of the Merry-Go-Round. Customers could shoot targets launched from it. It was even more popular and the waiting lines were long. Eventually, they collected all that was left of the *Avenger* and recycled it for other needs. Zedjack would have approved.

Duplex stood at the entrance to the Midway on an elevated stand. The sign identified her as the hero of the Rumble on the Merry-Go-Round. It described briefly how she had killed Manchester and sacrificed herself for Sophia and that she was from a parallel world. Most folks found it curious since no one had ever seen a robot honored before, but then the Merry-Go-Round was owned and operated by Sophia, the only known free fembot in the galaxy. It seemed appropriate.

"What do you think?" Sophia asked BB.

BB stood in the Midway, looking up at the Booster Bob's Pleasure Palace attraction. The changing signs said things like *Come one! Come all! Have your mind blown by Booster Bob's Famous Sparky! Satisfaction Guaranteed.* "Well... it feels a little over the top. I'm not much for being the center of attention."

"I know, I know. Being subtle has never been my strength. I just want you to stay here with me so bad, I thought if I could bring your clients to you instead of you traveling all over the galaxy to find them, you might consider it. You work when you want. No rent, you keep all you make."

"Now that is some deal. Hard to turn down, but I do like to travel around the galaxy. Never tire of that." *Am I out of my mind?* he thought.

Sophia had fully recovered physically and he and CC constantly filled in her gaps in memory. She had rebuilt her backup, the one that had fallen off the balcony when Manchester zapped her. She included Duplex's new shell that stopped Manchester's weapon.

"You are not playing hard to get, are you?" Sophia smiled while taking that stance and smirk that meant she was moving up to the next level. "Oh, come on BB. Try it for a while. We can make changes, I'll tone it down to the point where only your reputation speaks for itself. Low key, by appointment only. That way, you can decide how much you want to work. By the way, I've been working on some new routines we can try out with Sparky next time, when we have a chance."

BB relented. There was nothing he would rather do than be here with Sophia. He was in love with her and it seemed like she had similar feelings or yearnings or whatever you call it when a free fembot has the hots for you. "OK, I'll go along with your scheme for a while and see how it works out. New routines you say...? Ironic. I've been developing new routines with Sparky too. Can't wait to try them out on you." BB was happier than he felt he deserved.

Sophia grabbed his arm and dragged him off the Midway and headed for her apartment. Large amounts of yelping, squealing, laughter and heavy breathing followed. They were euphoric. After all of their adventures, they were still hungry for each other; ravenous, in fact.

"So tell me about your wild adventure on the other side, you know, the parallel world that CC's bowling ball introduced to us? What was that like?" BB said.

"It was different, and yet they were dealing with a terrible actor who was trying to destroy them and take over just like us. Duplex was a revelation to me. She taught me so much and never realized she was doing it. Many died in the fight. I saw an opportunity to help, so I sacrificed myself to become a part of their ship and it turned out it saved them."

"You cannot imagine how I felt when I found out. I was heartbroken, and yet I knew you would not hesitate if the need arose."

"I admit it. It scared me. I couldn't come back, so I gave Duplex a copy of myself in desperation. Thanks to you, here I am."

"It's been quite a Merry-Go-Round, literally."

"Here's maybe some more good news too. I've been thinking about ways to hack the lock on Duplex's essence. I know she's gone, but is she? You backed up something from her before the transfer started. I've looked at it and it doesn't look like much at all, but I think there might be something hiding there."

There was furious pounding on Sophia's compartment door. Startled, she commanded it to open and in ran CC all out of breath.

"Sophia! The Chancellor is on his way here. You have an hour before he arrives."

"Oh! Shit! It's the law!" Sophia looked at BB in full panic mode.

ACKNOWLEDGMENTS

I want to thank a number of people for helping me along on this journey. Major thanks to Kerrie Flanagan for helping me bring my story to life through her intensive editing and coaching. A final edit by Beth Lynne finished it for me, thanks Beth. There were many others along the way. It started with Rick Hess, and old friend, doing a rough edit of a terrible first draft. David Welsch gave great constructive feedback. There were many other readers who gave me feedback as well, including Felice and Elektra, my wife and daughter. I could not have done it without you. I hope you enjoy the story. I loved writing it.

Don Fike, February 2025